Diary of a SNOB

Also by Grace Dent

DIARY OF A CHAV

Trainers V. Tiaras

Slinging the Bling

Too Cool for School

Ibiza Nights

Fame and Fortune

Keeping It Real

DIARY OF A SNOB

Poor Little Rich Girl

Diary of a SNOB

Money can't buy me love

Grace Dent

A division of Hachette Children's Books

First published in Great Britain in 2010
by Hodder Children's Books

3

A Catalogue record for this book is available from the British Library

ISBN: 978 0 340 98975 3

Typeset in New Baskerville by Avon DataSet Ltd,
Bidford-on-Avon, Warwickshire

Printed in the UK by CPI Bookmarque, Croydon, CR0 4TD

The paper and board used in this paperback by Hodder Children's Books
are natural recyclable products made from wood grown in
sustainable forests. The manufacturing processes conform to the
environmental regulations of the country of origin.

Hodder Children's Books
a division of Hachette Children's Books
338 Euston Road, London NW1 3BH
An Hachette UK company
www.hachette.co.uk

For Mr Tom Gormer

This diary belongs to: Poppet Zanzibar Montague-Jones

Address: The fifth-floor TV den
1 Octavia Square
London NW5

DECEMBER

THURSDAY 31ST DECEMBER

6 P.M. 1 OCTAVIA SQUARE

POPPET ZANZIBAR MONTAGUE-JONES'S RUDDY IMPORTANT NEW YEAR'S RESOLUTIONS LIST

Resolution 1. VERY important. FIGURE OUT WHAT TO DO WITH RIDICULOUSLY GINORMOUS MOUNTAIN OF CASH COMING MY WAY SOON. Try to think of some sensible things to do with it involving Third World debt or poorly animals.

DO inform Mummy and Mr Chenowitz, the family accountant, that I was only joshing when I said I plan to buy Top Shop on Oxford Street, central London, then close it down every Saturday specifically to lark about IN THE NUDE trying on hats and faux-fur mufties and smear my bare behind along all the shiny surfaces. (Even if OBVIOUSLY this would be EPIC LOLZZ × one million.)

Stop claiming my ambition is to 'become a world-class cage fighter' or 'pay Cadbury's to sculpt a lifesized Dairy Milk version of Poppet so I can feel exactly what it's like to nibble my own boobs!' Silly talk like this only makes the grown-ups all swirly-eyed and shouty. NAUGHTY NAUGHTY POPPET!!

Resolution 2. TRY VERY VERY HARD TO GET ALONG WITH MY RUDDY IRRITATING BIG SISTER KITTEN MONTAGUE-JONES.

This year, we should try not to bicker so much and make Mummy all boo-hoo sad face. I should be happy that Kitten is now back home after Paradise Vision Rehabilitation Centre and has 'totally turned her back on the party lifestyle' and is hanging about Octavia Square all the ruddy time trying to 'like totally reignite the sister vibe between us'. Yes, even when she wakes me up at five a.m. to do Bliss-inducing Forest Yoga, which is basically doing headstands when it's still dark outside, and I have to witness her camel-toe in see-through yoga tights from varying explicit and eyewatering angles. This year, I need to try to listen to Kitten's advice about how 'it's great to be straight headed' without screaming, 'Oh shut it, Kitten, you ruddy hypocrite! When you were sixteen you spent every Saturday night at house parties in Chelsea, drunk out of your skull on Courvoisier, lying behind sofas while various male supermodels chewed your neck!' This year, I need to try to be calm when Kitten sticks her nose in my life and reports it all back to Mummy, and definitely STOP imagining how satisfying it would be to get my Kookaburra hockey stick and make the top of her head NICE AND RUDDY FLAT.

Resolution 3. HAVE SOME 'WORK' DONE.
Seriously. This year it's STARTING. I'm not letting Mother put me off this any longer. I need to fly off to one of Mummy's clinics in South Africa or somewhere and have some bits of my face swapped about a bit. I am so BORED with being ugly. Seriously, THE END. How can I carry on with this depressing collection of face appendages all just sat there in search of meaning on my face?! How? When I have VIXEN DIAZ-BROCKLEHURST as a best friend? Ruddy Vixen has been featured in the *Evening Standard* Top Ten Society Teen Goddesses spread AGAIN! And the photograph they used of her was a paparazzi shot, not a 'no make-up' one, or a stuffing her face with a Double Chocolate Krispy Kreme on Hampstead High Street WEARING GREY SWEATPANTS one. '*Effortless beauty, flawless style for the habitually chic Miss Vixen Diaz-Brocklehurst*' was what the caption said.

Well I'm done with effortless. Effortless is not working out for Poppet Montague-Jones. I'm old enough for a bit of nipping and tucking. Only subtle stuff though. Ears pinned back? Boob job? Nose shortened? Nothing too mental. Not like Della Carlton-Brown from our class at Hampstead Lycée for Young Ladies who disappeared off to Cape Town last summer and came back with a brow-lift, cheek implants and new bright-white front teeth. Lorks o' Lordy, I don't want to be mean but from certain angles she looks like a malevolent lifeforce from *Twilight*. Poor Della, apparently she's going back in spring to have her chin flattened and her nose re-set to even the whole look out. OUCH. I DON'T WANT THAT! I just want to look like normal girls – like the ones you see in magazines like *Teen Vogue*. IS THAT TOO MUCH TO ASK?

Resolution 4. HELP MY LITTLE BROTHER FLASH NIAGARA MONTAGUE-JONES WITH HIS FAMILY TREE PROJECT.

I need to be a GOOD sister and tell Flash, 'YES, I'd love to help you trace all the Montague family ancestors and YES I would especially love to map them out on one big enormous wall chart.' (Oh God, that sounds really complicated but if I don't say yes, he keeps setting off to the British Library all alone and climbing ladders to find books. HE IS SEVEN YEARS OLD.) I need to try to prepare Flash for the extreme unlikeliness that any of the Montague ancestors were 'noble warriors' or 'intrepid explorers' with names like 'Frederick the Fearless' or 'Tamrick the Tigerloin'. In fact if they're anything like Granny or Uncle Augustus they're more likely to be raging boozeheads called stuff like 'Reginald the Really-quite-drunk' and 'Bernhard the Blotto-by-Lunchtime'. I must prepare Flash for this sort of disappointment. It's like our Granny says after she's had her post lunch gin-and-tonic, 'The thing about the past, Poppet, is it's usually best left ruddy buried.'

Resolution 5. REMIND DRAGON ZINNAH MONTAGUE-JONES THAT HE IS ACTUALLY FROM LIBERIA IN AFRICA.

Oh, crikey this is annoying. According to this mental woman called Mrs Demansk down at the British Adoption Trust, the Montague-Jones family are not doing enough to 'honour Dragon's cultural roots'. Apparently, buying Dragon all those heaps of toys and clothes and stuff from Harrods and letting him sleeping in a nice nursery and not on a mattress with beetles crawling on his face will make him forget Mummy rescued him from an orphanage two thousand miles away. This is a bad thing apparently.

I hate Mrs Demansk. She's about fifty and wears bottle-green pop-socks under a brown shiny suit with an A-line skirt, and her glasses are covered in grease, which clearly obscures her view while she's NOSING AROUND OUR HOUSE WITH A CLIPBOARD.

'Dragon needs to know that he's different! He needs to remember he's African!' she said to us last week. Well, Mummy smiled calmly when she said that. (To be honest, I'd watched her take eighty grammes of Xanax about half an hour before she arrived so she was possibly rather fancying a lie down on the sofa wrapped in her leopard-skin slanket by this point.)

'Different?!' I tutted loudly. 'Dragon's got dark-brown skin and we're all porridge-coloured! I think he'll notice that! He's ADOPTED, NOT bloody BLIND!' Well, Kitten snorted Nespresso coffee down both nostrils then and Mummy told me to hush up. Why are grown-ups so utterly ANNOYING? It's only grown-ups who seem to notice what colour Dragon is.

Anyway, Kitten and I are rectifying matters forthwith by having African Days at Octavia Square featuring food, music and costumes. I asked Cyril, one of our chauffeurs from Nigeria (who I love very much, in fact I love him so much I sometimes call him Dad by mistake, which is jolly embarrasing) what Kitten and I would eat for supper if we were in Africa. Well, Cyril threw back his head and laughed when I asked that and said, 'Poppet, you never lift a finger to work in your whole life. In Africa you be going to bed with your belly EMPTY. In fact, in Africa your belly think your throat had been cut!' Then he laughed all the way from Octavia Square to my Renaissance Sculpture seminar at the Royal Academy of Art. I don't think I quite got the joke.

Resolution 6. TRY TO GET BACK IN MUMMY'S GOOD BOOKS AGAIN AFTER THE KWAME KOBINA INCIDENT.

I really need to smooth things over with Motherington after the whole 'secretly dating Kwame' thing. I need to stop her remarking to Daddy that I'm 'heading for trouble'. I really don't think I am. I'm ruddy boring. I'm a million miles from becoming 'Another Montague-Jones Wild Child,' which is what the *Daily Mail* helpfully said yesterday on pages four and five accompanied by a massive photo. A WILD CHILD? That ruddy photo was snapped in Paperchase while I was buying corrugated cardboard for Flash's family tree project. WOO-HOO PARTY HARD.

The newspapers are bitching about Mummy right now as my big brother Knute was arrested YET AGAIN this Boxing Day for doing one of his eco-warrior protests. This time Knute climbed over the security fence at Downing Street dressed as Santa Claus and left a present on the front doorstep of the Chancellor of the Exchequer's house.

It was a HUMAN POO! A turd in a tupperware box wrapped in sparkly snowman Christmas paper!

'I was making a protest about Third World water sanitation, Poppet!' Knute said when Daddy and I went to pick him up from West Central Police Station at three a.m. Mrs Minsk, our housekeeper, is rather vexed about her tupperware box. She said it was one of her favourites. I jolly well hope she throws it in the bin as I certainly won't be eating any of her homemade brownies out of it.

Anyway, the newspapers have gone BONKERS over the poo. In fact, there's about twenty paparazzi guys sitting on our front doorstep right now. Flash wants us to throw a poo at them too. Mummy got terribly irate when she heard that and said, 'NO more poos are being thrown or left by anyone, anywhere!' Then she put goody-two-shoes Kitten in charge of monitoring all our lavatory trips to make sure she heard us flushing. Daddy was very quiet. He just sat with his head in his hands at the kitchen table while Knute, Flash and Kitten bickered, then suddenly remembered an important business project he needed to sort out in the Los Angeles office which meant leaving Heathrow Airport at eight a.m. on THE FIRST OF JANUARY.

On balance, I think I am one of the BEST Montague-Jones kids.

The thing is, YES, OK, I know I screwed up this year with all that sneaking about with Kwame Kobina business. I KNOW I shouldn't have started hanging out at the Cottingham Estate, which according to my mother is A WAR ZONE populated by crackheads, rabid American pitbull terriers and Somalian gangsters. (It isn't really, it's in Kilburn, ten minutes away by bus. You can buy broadsheet newspapers and Camembert cheese in a shop quite near Kwame's flat so it's not completely horrid.) And the Cottingham Estate is actually sort of OK. It's a bit smelly and there's a few cracky weirdos hanging about, but mostly the people are nice. The thing was, I knew Mother would never believe that, so that's why I told all those lies. And Kwame is so utterly lush it didn't feel like I was doing anything wrong by being with him. How could anyone resist his big brown eyes and his brown skin and the way he laughs and . . . OH MY GOD, KWAME KOBINA IS AMMAAAAAAAAZING. I don't care if he's not a got a penny and he goes to a terrible school where they get frisked for guns and there's yellow Police Incident signs outside his house. I don't care. But Mother does care ENORMOUSLY about this stuff. And that's why I've told her that me and Kwame are over.

Sometimes I wish I'd never ruddy walked into McDonald's and set eyes on that boy. I said this to him this afternoon as a joke when we were whispering to each other on the phone about how crazy we are about each other. Kwame, being sensible as ever, says I need to go and tell my mother right away that he and I are back on. Kwame says I need to stop lying because lies create more lies and honesty is always the best policy. Kwame says my mother will have a little flip-out about how dangerous life is outside of Octavia Square but then she'll chill out. But I seriously can't face all that drama, so I've lied to Kwame that I'm telling her tonight, and I've told Mother that I've not spoken to Kwame for ages, and in actual fact my biggest decision is that this is the year when I'm having tremendous amounts of fun:

Resolution 7. DON'T GET RUDDY CAUGHT.

JANUARY

FRIDAY 1ST JANUARY

Oh heavens. Just been to Westminster Abbey with Granny for New Year Sung Eucharist and a sermon.

It turns out I am a SINNER.

The Archbishop was wiffling on about the importance of truth and about 'bearing false witness' and how it plummets sinners down into the firey furnace where wrong-doers live out eternity, thrashing about in a bath of BOILING HOT MARMITE while Satanic leprechauns feast on their bum cheeks. I may be paraphrasing slightly here. I tend to drift off a bit in church. Well if telling lies is a proper sin I'd better get ready for hell as I've started to find it rather good fun. I'M NOT PROUD OF THIS. But the fact is that lying is like being a secret agent. Like that *Bourne Ultimatum* bloke. You have one boring official life you tell everyone about . . . and then a whole different OTHER life full of one hundred per cent crashbangwallop naughtiness.

This is what I was thinking last night when Striker and Vixen and I were on the way home from our party. Not the party Mother threw here at 1 Octavia Square. The other party. The secret one I had to tell lies about. I am seriously considering rejecting Christianity if I'm not allowed to get up to stuff like this. I don't think Granny would be too upset. I think she only goes to Westminster Abbey and eats Communion Bread now and then as she's tremendous cocktail buddies with the Archbishop of Westminster, or 'Teddy' as she calls him. Teddy is terribly good about letting the Montague-Jones clan hold all our christenings and weddings and blessings and pet funerals in the big main fancy Abbey chapel, so even though the Montague-Jones family don't go to church much, the photos when we do can always sell for loads of money to *Hello!* magazine.

The party I was OFFICIALLY supposed to be attending last night was my parents' New Year's Eve cocktail bash. All my mother's friends and all the Octavia Square neighbours were invited. My mother's parties are really sort of legendary, well amongst grown-ups, who always say they are 'the social event of year' and are usually required to send bunches of orchids the next day to apologize for vomiting in the bath or trying to grope one of the *au pairs.* I'm not sure how grown-ups have the RUDDY CHEEK to say anything bad about teenagers because in my experience they only need the smallest SNIFF of vodka and they start acting like marauding Viking cannibals with ADD. And don't even get me started about the horrendous adult disco-dancing. My father only has one 'dance' that he does to every track, whatever the tempo or genre, which is running on the spot, shaking a pair of imaginary maracas, meanwhile my mother is prone to throwing both hands up in the air at the climax of songs screaming 'YES!!! COME ON!! MAKE SOME NOISE!' It is eyewateringly gruesome.

So by five p.m. last night, after the caterers and party planners had worked their magic on our house, it looked pretty much like a nightclub. There was a bar full of booze and a bartender in a white suit in almost every room downstairs and a marquee in the garden with disco glitter-balls hanging from the ceiling, like the ones you see in films of the olden days. The centrepiece of Mother's party was a freaky-looking two-metre-tall ice sculpture of Old Father Time made from of a block of frozen Russian vodka. Matthew, Mother's PA, had even paid some drama students to dress as woodland elves with pointy plastic ears to chip bits off and scoop them into plastic glasses with Tequila sauce for everyone to eat.

Poor Matthew had been driven insane sourcing oysters and sushi for two hundred people, plus a live performance from a Burlesque dancer called Miss Ruby Rozella, who was promising to swim around in a glass slipper full of champagne at midnight.

'Tsk! A ruddy stripper!' my sister Kitten said, when Ruby arrived and in our downstairs bathroom started putting on the bra she planned to take off again.

'It's BURLESQUE, Kitten!' my mother kept saying.

'Mother, just because she carries around two enormous feathers doesn't mean she isn't basically an oppressed sex-worker,' whined Kitten. 'I am registering my disapproval!'

I agreed a little bit, to be honest, but I tried to keep out of things. Kitten is jolly hard work now she's sober and has time to think about what she disapproves of. Kitten also disapproves of loud music (which might cause tinnitus), the free bar (which encourages binge drinking), and last night she even gave me and Mother a lecture on wearing high heels (which cause bunions and back problems). I think I preferred Kitten when I was visiting her whacked out of her head in Paradise Vision Rehabilitation Centre, when all she could be bothered to say was 'Splghh' and 'Gnnng' and 'Get me OUT OF HERE you bleeping ruddy bleepy bitch'. (Kitten used to curse like a trucker back then: ANOTHER THING SHE NOW DISAPPROVES OF.)

As I wandered through the midst of this chaos, Matthew intercepted me and tapped his clipboard. 'Poppet, note from your mother, you are not allowed any of the vodka sculpture. Jocasta said you're only allowed TWO UNITS of alcohol all evening.'

'Two units?' I spluttered. 'That's a small glass of champagne.'

'Indeed it is,' smiled Matthew, 'Happy New Year! Oh and by the way I've been asked to circulate your photograph to all the bar staff so they won't be serving you. Sorry.' Matthew checked to see I'd heard and then ticked it off on his clipboard.

'Oh whatevvvvver,' I said, rolling my eyes at him. 'The average age here is going to be, like, forty-five. I'm showing my face for ONE HOUR MAXIMUM and then going to my bedroom to watch a documentary about plankton. IT WILL BE MORE EXCITING.'

Matthew giggled lots when I said that. And at that point an argument was breaking out upstairs as a van had arrived with a dozen outdoor heaters for the marquee, which was making Knute very irate. 'Can't your friends put on extra coats and scarves,' spluttered Knute, 'instead of mutilating the OZONE!?'

Well, Mother laughed loudly at that then and said, 'Knute darling! If this party is anything like the ones I used to throw before you were born, well by midnight a lot of people won't be wearing any clothes at all! HA HA HA HA HA!'

I nearly sicked up my stomach lining through my tear-ducts when she said that. In fact, for the next hour the thought of Mother's wrinkly mates getting tipsy and actually 'doing it' around the back of the marquee kept playing over in my mind like a driller-torture scene from *Saw III*.

I wandered upstairs to Flash's room (or the Nerve Centre as he now likes to call it). Flash spends a lot of time in the Nerve Centre of late. Knute and I have an ongoing joke that Flash is planning to overthrow an African government or plotting a jihad. We giggle about this a lot. Secretly we just hope he's going to turn out normal as there's a lot of clever stuff going on in his tiny, little, white-blonde angelic head.

'Flashington,' I said.

'Poo-Pop Jellybelly,' he said, sitting up and pushing his glasses up his face.

'What's happening?' I said.

'Oh Grandad,' he said, casting a hand over his Ben 10 notepad on the floor.

'Oh yeah? What have you found out?' I said.

Flash has been finding out facts about our grandfather, Lord Edgar Montague, Granny's late husband. Grandpapa Edgar died before Flash and I were born. There's a large framed portrait of him from the 1950s on the fourth-floor balcony. He's dressed for a ball, his hair greased back and he's wearing a black tuxedo and smoking a cigarette, looking out of a window. Of late, I've started to realize Grandpapa was really rather handsome. He's got sharp cheekbones and beautiful lips. A lot like Knute. I am aware that admitting your grandfather and your big brother are both hotties is a million levels of wrongness.

I picked up a softwear box on Flash's bedroom floor. 'Aristocracy Unveiled: Genealogy Search,' I said. 'Was this what came from Amazon this morning?'

'Yes,' Flash replied.

OPEN A DOOR TO THE PAST! LET YOUR ANCESTORS COME FLOODING BACK! said the blurb on the back. That sounded rather terrifying to be honest. The last thing I need when I'm cleaning my teeth is ghosts of the Montague family popping up behind me howling, 'OH MY GOD WHY AM I SO DEAD? It is so BORING!'

'Lordy me, Flash, this won't end up with you sleeping upside down in my bed at three a.m. because yours is soaked in wee, will it?' I said.

Flash fixed me with one of his blood-curdling death stares. Pretty impressive for a person his size.

'Poppet, have you come to help me with my family tree or not?' he said.

'It's New Year's Eve!' I laughed. 'I told you we wouldn't do much today. Hey, are you going to change into your Spider-man pyjamasuit and clean your teeth? You can come down and say hello to the guests before you go to bed. You like doing that!'

Flash seemed not to hear me. He stared intensely at his laptop.

'I'm a child, not a performing monkey,' he said, after some silence.

'Oh, mmm, yeah obviously,' I said, trying not to crack up laughing. Sometimes I just want to grab him and nibble bits of him, he's so cute. 'Did you call Granny?' I asked. 'Did she say anything useful?'

'Yes, I called her,' said Flash, scrunching his brow. 'But she wasn't very helpful, to be honest. She just kept talking about how wonderful life used to be at De Beauvoir Manor, and that Grandpapa was "a true man of his time". And that his collection of Jaguar sports cars was world renowned. Oh and they had seven hundred acres of conifers.'

'Oh God, yes!' I said. 'The cars! Knute inherited the cars!'

'Where are they?' said Flash.

'Oh they're on loan to someone,' I said. 'I think they're in a museum in Saudi Arabia or somewhere. Knute isn't asking for them back just yet as it looks a bit dodgy with all his Save the Planet protests. Grandpapa gave them to Knute when he was still alive, Knute was only little. So we all wouldn't have to pay that inheritance tax thing on them.'

'What's inheritance tax?' said Flash.

'Oh, well,' I said, 'basically, if you die and you leave all your money and property to someone else, they can't have it unless they pay a massive amount of it to the government first. It's a tax. But we never pay it in our family as we've got Mr Chenowitz and he finds ways round it.'

Flash thought for a bit. 'But why are we different?' he said.

'Mmm,' I said, 'well I don't know. I suppose we just are. I don't suppose everyone else can afford accountants as clever as Mr Chenowitz.'

Flash wrote this down on his pad.

'Hey, I went to De Beauvoir Manor a few times,' I said. 'It was near Bath. I was only very little though. I don't remember much. Granny definitely had a lake and a family of swans. And in the middle of the lake was a tiny island with a little summerhouse and hammocks you could lie in on sunny days. Mother once told me that in the olden days Granny and Grandpapa used to make the servants fill little boats with champagne and hampers of lobsters and cheeses and row them all out to the island, then come back for them in the middle of the night when they were bladdered drunk.

'Really?!' said Flash.

'Yes!' I said. We started to laugh just thinking about it, but then I thought about the poor servants having to load all the booze fume grown-ups plus bottles and glasses into a boat and row back in the dark, and I felt quite bad.

'So do you remember about Granny selling the Manor?' Flash said.

'Not much,' I said. 'Grandpapa carked it, and then Granny was there alone in this massive twenty-bedroomed house, and I know the place was getting old and bits kept falling off it. I know one of the windows fell out of its frame and nearly killed a servant one day, which was like a major smell-the-coffee moment for Granny. And then Mr Chenowitz kept banging on about Granny opening up the east wing to the public and making a tearoom for tourists. Y'know, just to make the place worth keeping. But Mummy told me Granny said she'd rather throw petrol around and set the place alight and then burn it to the ground than let normal commoners traipse around in tracksuits chewing gum and scratching their private parts in the vicinity of her antique Persian rugs. So then she sold it to Americans and moved to Belgravia.'

Flash listened to this intently. It felt weird to be the one who actually knows some important facts. The only reason I know these things is because I am very, very nosy. I've spent all of my life pretending to be stupider than I am so I can hear grown-ups gossiping about stuff.

'So that's one generation sorted out then,' I said. 'Lord Edgar Montague, otherwise known as Grandpapa, married Granny. And they had three children: Mummy, Uncle Augustus and Aunt Alicia, then he died and that was that.'

Flash sighed. He didn't seem too satisfied with that. 'But what did he do all day?' Flash said.

'Whatever do you mean?' I said.

'For his whole life? What did Grandpapa do?' Flash said.

Now this stumped me a bit. 'Erm, I don't know. Hunting? Playing poker? That type of thing, innit?' I said.

Flash looked at me and rolled his eyes. 'Poppet, don't say *innit*,' he groaned, 'you sound ridiculous.'

My cheeks pinkened. I thought I sounded pretty street.

'He can't have just shot at grouse all of his life,' Flash said. 'There must be a secret story we don't know. Maybe he was an inventor? Or an explorer!'

I didn't say anything. This seemed unlikely. I don't

remember anyone on my mother's side of the family having a real job.

'It said in one of those books in the British Library,' Flash said, 'that in 1954 the Montague family owned property in Zambia in Africa. They owned a hunting lodge with two hundred acres. Did you know that?'

I was standing up now, trying to leave. This project was a bit of a headache already.

'Oh, erm, yeah,' I said, 'Grandpapa's brother, Charles, lived in Zambia for a while. Granny used to go out and stay there for months at a time. I've seen photos of them standing beside dead lions. And drinking martinis wearing safari suits.'

Suddenly I remembered something.

'Oh, hang on – JEWELS,' I said. 'Yeah that's right. Granny has a stack of Zambian emeralds in a vault. Like millions of pounds worth of them. The Victoria and Albert Museum once wrote a piece in *The Times* slagging Granny off because she won't lend them the emeralds to put on show.'

'Zambian emeralds?' Flash said. 'Do you know how she got them?'

'I don't know,' I said. 'I just know she's got a ton of them. Really old, big ones. The Zambian government know she's got them, as they once wanted to fly someone over to look at them, but she told them to bugger off.'

I wanted to change the subject now. It was making me feel uncomfortable. How does Granny have all of this stuff?

I wondered whether Granny even owned the emeralds now. Maybe I owned them? Why do I not listen more in Mr Chenowitz's office?

'Is Karina staying to look after you tonight?' I said to Flash.

Flash checked the iCalendar that he syncs with Mummy's laptop. 'Yes, she's twenty-three minutes late already,' he said.

'Ha! Are you going to grass her up?' I laughed.

'Don't be silly, Poo-Pop,' said Flash, 'I love Karina. Karina's one of my favourite people in the whole wide world.'

I laughed when he said that. My mother hates it when Flash says that. It drives her ruddy insane.

It was seven-thirty p.m. and I still hadn't decided on a New Year's Eve outfit. It's things like this that make me think I am a peculiar type of girl. Not like Vixen and Striker, who had plotted every item of their entire whole look days ago and, according to my iChat screen, were currently arranging for Striker to bring spare false eyelash glue as Vixen had ran out. *POPPET ARE YOU THERE? ARE YOU ONLINE?* they'd both kept asking before resorting to just posting joke abuse about me accompanied by many *LOLZ*.

Vixqueen: *POPZ HAS GIVEN UP ON FALSE EYELASHES* AFTER LAST DISASTER.

Strikezone 100: *LOLZZZ OH YEAH. I WONT ASK HER.*

They were right, of course, I *have* given up with false eyelashes after last year's Hampstead Lycée for Young Ladies/Godspeed Boys' Academy mixer when the one on my left eye got loose and slid down my face, resting on my top lip. I didn't notice for TWO WHOLE SONGS until Marmaduke Adams saw it and shouted, 'Hey EVERYONE, Poppet's moustache is really getting bushy these days! I think her hormone pills are starting to work! Nearly time for the sex change, Percy!! Show us your wanger! HAHAHAHAHA!'

I hate Marmaduke Adams, he is a RUDDY BIG PIG. I was starting to get stressed now just thinking about going out in public. I had absolutely no idea what to put on that night to fit with where I was going.

The next thirty minutes were a blur of pulling footless tights on, then pulling them off again, and wriggling into dresses, and walking up to the mirror and casually waving at myself trying to imagine what I'd look like when I made my big entrance. I tried a pale sea-green Ghost floaty mini-dress over midnight-blue footless tights and Gucci pumps with a black Pashmina around my shoulders.

'Hello I'm Poppet!' I waved at the mirror. 'Ugh,' I groaned to myself, 'You look sooo Hampstead. They'll EAT YOU ALIVE.'

I found my little black soft-leather biker jacket then swept my hair up into a top ponytail that stretched my face a bit like the girls in Kilburn.

'Hello! I'm Poppet, innit, enchanted to meet you! BRAP!' I said.

I looked mental. Suddenly the New Year's Eve party Kwame had invited us to seemed like a very bad idea.

'Paloma, DAAAAAARLING, come in!!' I heard Mother screaming downstairs, welcoming Striker's mother through the door. 'Oh look! My neighbours have come *en masse*! Frangipan! Henry! Persephone! Felix! Come in! Salutations of the season to you all! OH MY WORD, STRIKER, WHAT HAVE YOU DONE TO YOUR HAIR!? I thought you liked it BLUE!?'

There was a thundering of feet on the spiral staircase and then Vixen and Striker fell giggling through my bedroom door screaming, 'HELLLLLLLLLLLLOOOO OOOOOOOOOOOOO!'

I took a step backwards in shock at Striker's hair. It was cropped really short into an elfin cut and she'd dyed it WHITE. In fact it was so white it was almost SILVER!!

'What the . . . ?!' I said. 'You . . . you . . . look like a CYBORG!'

'Isn't it amaaaaazing?' Striker hooted. One of her boobs was already escaping from the black bra underneath her opaque lace dress.

'Best one yet so far?!' said Vixen. Vixen's hair was backcombed into a loose beehive and pinned with silver bumble-bee clips up the back. She looked stunning. Like a supermodel who'd just run through a beehive on her way to the MTV Video Awards' red carpet. 'Oh my God! Looking HOT Popsicle,' said Vixen, pointing at my outfit.

'Really?' I said.

'YES!' my friends both chorused.

'Hang on, didn't Felix arrive with you?' I said. I couldn't hear his footsteps on the stairs. I was expecting him to drift up to my room and laugh at us getting ready.

'Oh yeah,' said Striker. 'He says he's only staying an hour. He has another cocktail party to be at.'

'Who's party?' I said, raising an eyebrow, and then I remembered I had no right at all to wonder about my good friend Felix's life. The fact is I've not paid him a terrible amount of attention since I met Kwame. I suspect Felix may be a tad narked with me. Or maybe I'm just imagining this. Maybe he doesn't care at all. Oh I wished my brain would stop whirring and clanking.

'Listen, Pops,' Vix said, 'how long do we have to stay downstairs so it doesn't look suspicious? 'I'm not being a diva but my father's last words to me as I was leaving the house was that he "was putting on his dancing trousers and getting ready to boogie on down".'

'Oh dismalness,' I groaned, 'I am so stopping partying when I hit thirty years old. It's totally unfair to your children, isn't it?'

'Oh I'll never be thirty anyway,' said Striker, lying down on my bed, 'I'd rather just party hard for the next ten years and see where that takes me. You know, go out with a bang when I'm twenty-nine!'

I pretended not to hear that. Striker says dramatic things about getting old an awful lot. We tend to just ignore her. The other day she said that she was going to take herself off to a Swiss clinic and make them kill her the very second she started thinking sensible mum jeans were vaguely OK.

'Look,' Striker said, 'a car is picking us up at ten p.m. from here. And another one is coming at twelve-fifteen a.m. to bring us home. I booked them on my mother's account; she never checks it and she'll have a hangover for a week anyway. There's no way anyone will miss us.'

'Hmmm,' I said, suddenly feeling really nervous.

'Oh bloody chill out, Pops!' giggled Striker. 'We're going to a party, not doing an armed robbery. Anyway, MORE IMPORTANTLY, what are Kwame's friends down the Cottingham Estate like? Are any of them hot? I want a New Year's Eve snog and I'm not that fussy.'

'STRIKER! Haahahahahahahaha,' giggled Vixen, putting on more lipgloss. 'You're awful. I LOVE IT.'

'Striker, you are NOT getting off with anyone from the Cottingham Estate!' I said firmly. 'No way. We go to the party, we say hello, you meet Kwame properly, we look sociable, we come home, bish bash and bosh! THE END. Don't get off with anyone. PLEASE.'

'Why not?' said Striker, looking totally discombobulated by this request.

'Because . . .' I spluttered. 'Because . . . There are some MENTAL people in the Cottingham Eatate! That's why!'

'Oh my word, Poppet, you sound just like your mother!' howled Striker, kicking her tiny size three feet in the air, enjoying this a great deal.

'NO!' I said. 'No . . . not like that . . . Listen, Kwame is sweet and lovely and the people I've met through him are wonderful, but it's . . . it's still the ruddy Cottingham Estate, you need to be careful.'

'Poppet,' said Striker, looking fake-shocked, 'is it because a lot of the people on the Cottingham Estate are . . . black people?? You are SUCH a racist!'

My eyes narrowed, falling right into her trap. 'STRIKER! HOW CAN I BE A RACIST?! I'M IN LOVE WITH A RUDDY BLACK BOY!?'

'Ahhh, but maybe you're only doing it to COVER your racism?' gasped Vixen, raising a perfectly plucked eyebrow.

'Yes, that's the first sign of a racist isn't it?' nodded Striker, 'claiming NOT to be one. What a shame. Poppet, this is shocking news.'

'Oh shut up, the ruddy pair of you,' I said, shaking my head, realizing they were winding me right up. They were both hooting with laughter at my little red face and outraged expression.

'Poppet,' said Striker suddenly, 'what's it like to kiss a black boy? I mean, I kissed Kenny Lim from Godspeed once but I don't know if that counts.'

'Striker, he's half-Korean, quarter-Scottish, quarter-Ethiopian,' said Vixen, 'I don't think he counts.'

'He's a gigantic boring fart,' said Striker. 'I shall not be revisiting, I know that. No, I mean properly black, Popz.'

I thought for a second. And then a big smile must have spread all over my face. 'It's . . . like, ughhh, ammmmazing,' I said. 'In fact, it's—'

'Actually, STOP,' said Striker, holding up her palm flat. 'Don't spoil my surprise, I'm going to find out myself AT MIDNIGHT.'

Vixen started giggling again, even louder this time.

'Oh *whatever*,' I said. 'Come on, let's go downstairs and be good daughters for a few hours. Everyone do their best angelic smile!'

We all smiled at each other in the most lame manner imaginable. Then we headed out of the bedroom door downstairs, where my mother was shouting, 'COME ON EVERYONE MAKE SOME NOISE!' already.

Our driver wasn't enormously keen on even going near to the Cottingham Estate, let alone letting three girls out of the car unaccompanied. But after a few long, awkward silences he eventually rolled his eyes and parked in front of the estate's rather grotty community hall with the broken-down wall in front of it and the doors and windows covered in grafitti and clumsy spray paintings of willies and guns, plus one new addition to the mess I'd never noticed before: a line of Nazi swastikas painted in bright-yellow paint with the slogan *BNP FOREVER PAKIS OUT*. I've only recently heard about these BNP people as

Kwame told me about them, and suffice to say they are not entirely pleasant – in fact they are HORRIBLE RACIST PIGS.

I stood for a moment realizing how the Cottingham Estate must look to Striker and Vixen, seeing it all for the first time. I felt a bit ashamed and wished it could have all looked a bit tidier. I wanted Vixen and Striker to know that no matter how many times Kwame complains to the council and makes them paint over the rude words some idiots from the Sook Hill Estate ride down on mopeds and spray paint it again. The police seriously don't seem to give a damn either, which is mad, because at Octavia Square Daddy once managed to get a paparazzi guy fined two thousand pounds simply for leaving a kebab box on our front doorstep. Daddy had the man prosecuted for criminal damage! I don't understand why no one gets prosecuted for smashing up the Cottingham Estate. It's like the police have sort of given up.

Outside Cottingham Hall about thirty boys and girls were hanging out chatting and smoking fags. A few Staffordshire bull terrier dogs were running loose barking and play-fighting. A pale-green lazer was flashing madly from inside the hall and a really heavy bassline was rattling the pavement.

'Shall we just go in?' Vixen said. She seemed very subdued. Meanwhile Striker was staring at the scene before us with crazy, wild, spinning pupils. Her mouth was open in a perfect O as she FIZZED WITH

IMPATIENCE to rocket herself straight into the middle of whatever was happening inside that hall. Vixen, on the other hand, seemed to have shrunk to almost half her size.

'Come on, Vix,' I said, sliding my arm through hers to try and pull her along.

As we clomped ahead in a wall of three towards the crowd, everyone seemed to stop and stare. I scanned the crowd, trying to work out who I knew already to say hello to, but it was dark and lots of the boys were wearing their hoods up so it was pretty hard and, to be quite frank, most of girls were completely unrecognizable as they were TRANSFORMED into totally different entities by their New Year's outifts.

Suddenly I realized one of the girls was Shazzalla, Kwame's friend who helps him with the events he puts on at the Cottingham Estate. Shazzalla couldn't have looked more New Year's Eve if she tried. She had on a tiny gold skirt with bare legs and high silver heels. Her pale white enormous boobs were almost hanging out of an itsy-bitsy pink vest top and her hair was sculpted and sprayed into fierce arrangements, and she was wearing tons of fake bling. Shazalla was laughing with her mates Jezzebella and Shaquilla. The Cottingham girls looked AMAZING but inside my head all I could hear was Blitzen Trapper from my class at Hampstead Lycée laughing till she nearly peed in her Coco La Mer thong at them because the only label the Cottingham girls wear is Primark and lots of them do crazy stuff like shave the sides of their heads then clip their baby's initials into the stubble and say: 'Ere Poppet, I worship the bones of that kid, iznit? I'm gonna have his name in my hair for now . . . until I can save up for the tattoo on my bum.' I never really know what to say to that so I do what Granny does when she's flummoxed and go, 'How divine!'

'Aight, Poppet? DUCHESS!?' Shazalla screamed at me, 'Ahhh, you linked innit! Whozedatden then? You rollindeeptonight? Ere we got a bit of class down the Cottingham, girls!'

'Hello, Shazzalla!' I said. 'Yes, I'm here!'

'Sick! Hahaha! Kwame said if you didn't show he was gon be vex!' laughed Shazzalla. 'Ere, al text him nahh innit!'

'*What is she saying?*' whispered Vixen. 'Is she speaking English?'

'Shhh,' I whispered back, nudging her arm to be quiet. 'Shazzalla is texting Kwame to say we're here.'

'Hello, I'm Striker!' said Striker, introducing herself as I quite rudely hadn't. Suddenly Striker's voice sounded all harsh and clipped, a bit like when Granny's friends talk about why it's a human being's God-given right to shoot elephants.

'Wot you say? *Striker!?*' Shazzalla said, popping her phone back between her boobs. Shazzalla is famous for keeping things she wants to keep safe – purse, phone etc – between her knockers. Shazzalla says there are some pretty skilful thieves on the Cottingham Estate but she challenges ANYONE to actually get anything from between her boobs without her knowing. This is a highly salient point.

'Yes, Striker!' confirmed Striker. 'And this is Vixen!'

'Enchaaaanted to meet you,' said Vixen.

I cringed. Why do we all say that? It makes no sense. How can you be enchanted by meeting anyone? Enchanted means 'mystified' or 'bedazzled' or 'rendered incapable of sensible thought', yet over at Octavia Square we say it all the time. Even to the person who has come to pick our dry cleaning up. I could feel myself getting smaller by the second worrying what Shazzalla thought of my friends and what my friends thought of the Cottingham Estate and worrying that all the worrying was spoiling New Year's Eve.

'So, hang on,' says Shazzalla. 'Youiz Striker? And youiz Vixen, iznit? Oh my dayzz!' laughed Shazzalla. 'You posh birds have got some well messed-up names! Your folks must have been trippin!'

Shazzalla was giggling like mad now. She poked one of her friends standing with her back to us. 'Ere, Oceanspray?!' she said.

A rather plump mixed-race girl in barely-there black mini-skirt that showed her muffin top and her bum cheeks, span round.

'Oceanspray, this is Vixen and Striker!'

'Oceanspray?!' Striker said in my ear. 'That's a brand of cranberry juice!'

'Shut up, Striker,' I said, kicking her ankle.

Just that minute Kwame appeared, THANK GOD, looking enormously GORGEOUS in a navy-blue soft lambswool jersey, which really suited his broad shoulders and LUSCIOUS brown skin, with dark navy jeans and new white Nikes. For once Kwame had spent some of his Christmas cash on something other than school books. I didn't know whether to feel proud about that or guilty for leading him astray, but I was going with proud, as my boyfriend looked so unbelievably freaking crazy HAAAAWWT.

'Duchess!' he said, curling his arm around my waist and kissing my ear, nuzzling his face in my hair to smell my perfume. I wanted to lie down on the pavement and laugh hysterically, waving my ankles about, as I was so insanely happy.

'Kwame, you remember Vix and Striker, don't you?' I said. 'You met them outside the school last year?'

The girls both stared dumbstruck at Kwame. I've seen him have this effect on girls before. I don't think Kwame has really any idea how HOT he is. That's one of the best bits about him.

'I've heard a lot about you,' Kwame said smiling.

'Probably lies, Poppet is terrible for that,' Vixen said, visibly cringing.

'Oh I don't know,' said Kwame mischievously. 'You're the girl who gave all that money to the charity to save the Argentinian street cats?'

'Oh . . . erm . . . yes, that was me,' laughed Vixen, looking a bit sheepish, although I don't know why, as she'd do it again tomorrow if her father hadn't changed all the passcodes on her trust fund bank account:

Kwame shook his head and smiled, then said to Striker, 'And you got suspended last term for dying your hair red?'

'Oh yeah! Three weeks. Just for dying my hair. What a complete bunch of facists. I hate that crappy school.' Striker's eyes were swivelling round, checking out all of the passing boy talent.

A black Golf GTI had just pulled up and five boys had jumped out, slamming doors, wearing deadly serious expressions. Kwame's face definitely tensed as a tall guy with light-brown skin, a shaved head and dark-brown mid-length fur coat a bit like a 70s' pimp would wear crashed the driver's seat door shut, bleeped the central locking and walked towards the hall. He looked straight at Kwame and nodded and Kwame nodded back, but they didn't exactly seem like friends.

'I don't care whether they expel me for good,' said Striker, 'I bloody hate that place.'

'Anyway!' I said, quickly trying to change the subject. I knew Kwame didn't really want to hear us slagging off our rather expensive private all-girls school, with its amazing space-age science labs and specialist teachers who coach us for Oxford Uni, and its helicopter pad on the roof for when our parents want to do the school run from our holiday villas in Tuscany and the Algarve. At Kwame's school the supply teacher appears to think they've achieved something if pupils leave with a thorough knowledge of the alphabet and the ability to write their name all in one line without abbreviating it into text speak and finishing it with 4EVVVVA.

'Your mother know you're here?' Kwame asked me.

'Oh, yeah,' I lied, 'I had a chat with her before. We're all good.'

Kwame looked relieved. Vix and Striker pretended not to hear. 'Oh that's the best news I've heard for ages!' he said.

Something inside me squelched with guilt. There was no way I was telling my mother where I was going tonight. She'd have locked me in the cellar and hidden my wardrobe.

'Shall we go inside?' I said.

'Yeah, come on,' said Kwame.

'Let's go!' said Striker, leading the way towards the hall door. As she stepped through the crowd of boys near the front door, they seemed to split in half leaving a path through the middle.

'Who the hell is dat, Kwamms?' one boy with cornrow dreads drooled, pointing at Striker. 'She is crazyhot.'

Cornrow boy stuck his hand out to touch Striker's hand and pull her backwards towards him. Striker allowed him take her hand softly, then she looked back behind her and into his eyes, before sliding her fingers out of his reach and walking away with a wiggle of her neat little bum, finally dropping her hand and never looking back, as if the whole thing had never happened at all. This is the sort of boy entrancing manoeuver that Striker Earhart excels at. Tiny, subtle, sexy things like this that drive boys KRAZZZYMENTALINSANE. If I tried to do this, I'd no doubt get my bracelet caught in the boy's jumper then walk for twenty metres with wool unravelling until he was stood there looking angry with his nipples freezing off. SERIOUSLY, I am the anti-sex. I visualize myself living with my elderly parents and a collection of labradors, still COMPLETELY A VIRGIN when I'm thirty-eight. I don't know how I lucked out with Kwame.

'Kwame,' I whispered, 'is there a bar in there?'

'Nah, some of the kids have brought cans in, but we tried to stop them,' he said.

'Ah, OK,' I said. 'It's just, y'know Striker? It's best to not to let her have any booze. She goes a bit, erm, mental.'

'Oh, OK, don't worry,' said Kwame, 'I don't think there's much booze in there anyway. I'm keeping this party on the right side of the law. I can't have the community centre shut down just as we've got that charity grant for the new roof. This is the beginning for the Cottingham, not the end!'

I smiled to myself a little bit when he said that. I'll never tell him why . . .

* * *

The hall was rammed with bodies. It was almost pitch black aside from the lazer and a few twinkling Christmas grotto lights along the walls. Within seconds of reaching the dancefloor Striker had vanished. I looked around me frantically but she'd totally gone. VAMOOSH. I tried to relax and wiggle to the music a bit in a suitable carefree fashion, but the fact was I'd managed to lose Striker and she's not the sort of girl you want to lose on the Cottingham Estate – in fact the thought of going home without her was starting to give me sudden impact eczema around the backs of my knees. Just then Shazalla and her friends appeared and the DJ dropped in a dancehall track that everyone seemed to know except me and suddenly – HOSANNAH – I caught sight of Striker dancing at the other side of the room. She was waving her arms in the air and chucking back a can of Red Stripe lager, lost in the bassline with her eyes shut and her waist winding perfectly in time with the rhythm. In the pale-green strobe light Striker's skin looked like porcelain and her hair like bacofoil. She turned and passed the can of lager back to the boy beside her. It was that tall boy with the fur coat who was driving the car. As Striker shook her bum in his general direction, the boy took a lighter out, flicked it and put the flame right up to Striker's face.

Kwame noticed me looking rather shocked as I turned and grabbed his arm. He said, 'What's up, Duch?'

'Him. Over there with Striker? What's he doing with that lighter?!' I said. The boy had let the flame die now and was putting it back in his pocket.

'What, oh him?' said Kwame, rolling his eyes. 'It must be too dark for Bizzle to see what Striker's face is like. So he's just double-checkin' whether she's butterz or not before he makes his move.'

CHECKIN' WHETHER SHE'S BUTTERZ? BUTTERZ, AS IN UGLY?? WHAT A RUDDY CHEEK!

I opened my mouth to say something then clamped it closed again. I could hardly start complaining about how RUDE and SEXIST this Bizzle boy was when Striker seemed perfectly content with the situation. In fact, having passed Bizzle's test, Striker was sticking her hands inside his fur coat and reaching up underneath his top to touch his bare chest.

Kwame frowned when he saw that.

'Why's he called Bizzle?' I asked.

His name's Julius Bisley.' Kwame didn't say anything for a few seconds. 'I'm not exactly friends with him. I didn't think he'd come down here. Bizzle's never out after seven at night. He's not allowed.'

'Oh,' I said, 'are his parents very strict?'

I cringe thinking about this now. I must have sounded like an utter numbskull.

'No, Duchess,' Kwame said. 'He's got a tag.'

'A skin tag?' I said. 'Like a mole on his skin? Oh you can have them removed. My mother's got an excellent surgeon who took one off her neck! It's a one-hour job on Harley Street.'

Kwame looked confused. 'A TAG on his ankle, Poppet!' he said. 'An electronic tag. From the police. He's on a curfew. Maybe it's finished now. Either that or he's breaking the law being here. I could seriously do without the police appearing. That's not what we need.'

'Oh,' I said. I looked at my watch, it was ten to midnight and I didn't feel much in the party mood, not one little bit.

'Why has Bizzle got a tag?' I said.

'Errrm . . . shottin Charlie I think,' said Kwame, matter of factly.

I swear I felt my blood go cold.

'He shot Charlie!!' I said. 'Who's Charlie?'

'No, not like that,' Kwame said. 'Shottin? Y'know, selling stuff? Charlie? Charlie means cocaine.'

Sometimes when I meet Kwame on his home turf it feels like we're speaking two completely different languages. Like when I tell him about things from Hampstead Lycée and he laughs and says it sounds like I'm telling him about something from *Harry Potter.*

'Bizzle was selling drugs, basically. For his older brother. His brother went in Brixton jail for five years. Bizzle just got a tag.' Kwame thought for a second. 'Thing is, Duch, he's sort of all right deep down. He's just got on the wrong path. Brother's not thinkin' straight.'

'Hmmm,' I said. I looked over at Striker and Bizzle, who were flirting like mad. They were sharing a cigarette. Striker doesn't smoke. I glared in her direction and bit my lip hard, just as Vixen grabbed my hand and shook it furiously.

'Poppet! Look at the expression on you!' she said. 'It's New Year's Eve! Good vibes, OK? It's almost midnight already! Let's just have a good time for half an hour then we'll rescue Striker and leave. Let it go, Pops. Striker does whatever she wants no matter what we say!'

Right then the DJ dropped in a track I definitely did know called 'Sweat Ya Perm Out' by L'il Jon. Kwame, Vixen, Shazzalla, Oceanspray, Jezebella and Shaquilla propelled themselves right into the middle of the floor and when the first verse started with 'I ain't never seen a booty so fat. It's all hangin' out the back of yo pants!' well, the room stated going insane, particularly Shazzalla, who was leaning right forward, pushing her bum cheeks straight up into the air, waggling her arse back and forth. I know Shazzalla would not mind me saying that she has quite a generous posterior so this was QUITE A FORMIDABLE SPECTACLE TO BEHOLD.

All the kids dancing round us were screeeeeaming and shouting 'Shazzz-alla! Shazzz-alla! Shazzzzzalllla!'

Well, right then Shazalla dropped almost to the floor on her knees, then jumped back up onto her haunches with her knees apart and started doing like a weird lapdance trick, raising her body up slowly in time to the beat, wobbling her bum cheeks at extra-fast speed.

Everyone was SCREAMING! Shazalla could really do this move like someone out of a L'il Jon video! in fact I think this was the exact point that the party really actually BEGAN. It felt like everyone seemed to pull together all at once and the atmosphere just flipped over from quite serious to suddenly very seriously fun, and just right then I started thinking how music is quite bizarre because no matter how different we all are as people, when we're all on a dancefloor with a tune we like playing loud, well basically we're all the ruddy same.

And I was thinking as the bells chimed and everyone was shouting 'Happy New Year!': Gosh, wouldn't the earth be a lot jollier and wouldn't GCSE History be less ruddy depressing and full of wars if people had thrown more parties instead of killing each other in vast numbers over things that don't even matter. I thought that maybe one day I shall go into politics and start my own political party called the Poppet Montague-Jones: Let's Have More Parties Party!

I tried to communicate this to the girls on the way home but sometimes I'm not terribly good at expressing my more profound thoughts so instead I said, 'That party was bare good innit?'

And instead of correcting me or saying, 'Don't talk like that, Poppet, you sound silly,' Striker just smiled dreamily and said, 'Popz, that shubz was baregooood. Bellzy is so CHOONG!'

Well we all giggled when she said that, even our driver, who turned up Heart FM for us and let us sing along to cheesy 90s' songs all the way home. In fact the vibe in the car was so good it seemed churlish to inform Striker that I'd already decided I was NEVER LETTING HER GO NEAR THE COTTINGHAM ESTATE EVER, EVER AGAIN.

THURSDAY 7TH JANUARY

Oh LORDY LORDY ME, HOW I LOATHE SCHOOL. Seriously. Loathe it. It is hell. And to make matters more beastly, these days I can only write these feelings of contempt here in my diary. Because every time my boyfriend, Kwame Kobina, mentions GCSEs and A-levels and how keen he is to stay in education until he's at least one hundred and five years old, well I have to pretend to be a swot too and say stuff such as, 'Gosh, I totally agree, Kwamikins! Expanding the mind is like soooo utterly crucial.' And then I have to pull a face as if I've just remembered something exciting about quantum physics, which Kwame loves, and even wants to watch bloody documentaries about on BBC iPlayer instead of EastEnders. Kwame gets very discombobulated when people don't fully comprehend that trying hard at school is CRUCIAL TO YOUR FUTURE HAPPINESS and he certainly doesn't like it when I say things like, 'Oh Kwame, CHILL! Maybe I want to be an idiot! Maybe there's a strong argument in this world that happiness lies in being a buffoon! In fact, my Aunty Alicia is a complete buffoon and she is BLISSFUL. Alicia thinks the moon is about two kilometres up in the air and made of sand and that Africa is a country next to Asia, and she's the happiest person I know! In fact Kwame, sometimes I think the more knowledge one has, the more things there are to worry about. Maybe I would rather be thick and joyful!'

I told Kwame this on iChat this evening and there was such a long silence after I pressed return that I ended up quitting then reopening the iChat application as I thought it must be stuck.

Eventually Kwame typed: *You're joking with me right?*

Yes, of course, MEGA LOLZ, I love school really, I typed quickly, *ROFL! DON'T TAKE ME SO SERIOUSLY!*

So much for bloody freedom of speech. I am living a lie.

I don't want Kwame to know that my first week back at Hampstead Lycée has been spine-chillingly dismal.

For example, a low point for me today was English Literature where we're studying *Wuthering Heights* by Emily Brontë. OH MY GOOD LORD, IT IS BORING. Vixen says it's one of the greatest books in the world but in fact it is quite literally two emotional retards running backwards and forwards across a windy hill shouting for forty years going, 'Ooh I fancy you!' and 'Ooh so do I' and 'Gosh this hill is breezy!' And this goes on for four hundred pages until one of them carks it. Lorks o' Lordy me, it takes all my energy to keep both of my eyes focused on the same page without one of them rebelling and saying, 'Oh bugger this to high heaven, I'm going for a kip.'

Vixen says I am mad. Vixen loves *Wuthering Heights* so much she's already proclaimed it life-changing and spent a lot of today's double lesson dabbing her eyes wimpering stuff such as, 'Gosh, Cathy's unrequited yearning for the man she loves is sooo enormously traaaagic!'

Striker laughed like a drain when Vixen said this, then said, 'The main idea I'm picking up is that this Heathcliff must have one extra enormous trouser-sausage.'

'Striker!' said Vixen, violated by the idea. 'There are no trouser-sausages in *Wuthering Heights*! It's a trouser-sausage-free book! It's about longing and yearning to see a trouser-sausage but very rarely ever doing it.'

'Gnnn, yeah,' tutted Striker, 'that's why it's crap. That's where this Brontë woman went wrong. What's the ruddy point of slogging through three hundred pages of people wanting to do stuff then never getting round to it. That's why I only read Jackie Collins. Everyone is just doing it in every chapter. DOING IT ALL THE TIME EVERYWHERE!'

'So this Garfield guy has an enormous thingy!?' I said, really trying to keep up. 'I missed that bit.'

Vixen looked at me oddly.

'Who's Garfield, Poppet?' Striker said.

'Garfield,' I said. 'The main guy. The one who loves Cathy.'

'There's no one in the book called Garfield, Poppet,' said Vixen.

'Yes there is!' I said. 'Him who lives in the house who's always in a strop.'

'*Heathcliff*,' Vixen corrected me.

'*Heathcliff*? What, are you sure?' I said. 'Oh God . . . Oh . . . oh, oh *gngngn*.' The essay I'd just handed in was looking suddenly rather confusing.

Striker was laughing really hard by this point.

'No, hang on, Pops!' she said. 'There IS a Garfield in *Wuthering Heights*. Definitely. Ginger-haired? Whiskers. Furry tail? He's always asleep. Or eating lasagna!'

I could feel a puddle of bum-cleft sweat forming by this point. It was far too late to get the essay back.

'Striker! Don't confuse Poppet any further!' said Vixen. 'We need to help her. Poppet, you wrote that essay in the car this morning, why did you not just double-check the name with us?'

'Poppet,' butted in Striker, 'you need to FINISH the book. Can you not get yourself excluded for a few days and stay in bed and read it!'

'IGNORE HER!' said Vixen. 'No one is getting excluded! Stop making me stressed, both of you. I had acupuncture in my ears yesterday. You're totally harshing the mellow.'

'Sorry, Vix,' said Striker, trying not to giggle.

'You've got to read the book, Popz,' said Vixen, quietly.

'I know.' I sighed.

The truth is that all I appear to be doing in the 'crucial run up to the GCSE period' is thinking about Kwame. His eyes or his voice – or his bum, more specifically. Or planning where we'll live in Africa when he goes there to become a fever doctor and I'm Mrs Poppet Kobina. Or worrying how much Mother will have a major crap-attack when I email her Blackberry in Valencia and admit I'm still seeing that boy from THE COTTINGHAM ESTATE. In fact, the most productive thing that I've achieved this term so far was collecting a lot of boiled egg shells from Mrs Minsk's compost box then crushing them and gluing them into a picture of Humpty Dumpty for Flash's Art homework. I did this in return for him doing my Algebra homework. I'm doing quite well in Maths so far this term. How peculiar.

FRIDAY 8TH JANUARY

Striker has taken up smoking again. REALLY SMOKING. This time she seems seriously devoted to her hobby, unlike in Year Nine when she'd chug and cough her way through half a Marlboro Lite then throw up in a wheeliebin and need to sit down due to dizziness.

This time Striker has mastered the art of puffing neat smoke rings and double-drawing the fag smoke back into her mouth then blaring it down both nostrils. She thinks she looks sexy. I think she looks like Bilbo Baggins from *Lord of the Rings* puffing on a pipe at a Shire tea-party, but who listens to me these days? NOBODY, THAT'S WHO.

Striker keeps forcing Vixen and I to walk the long way to to lessons around the back of the sports halls so she can top up her nicotine levels and make her lungs nice and black and crispy. It's a bit of a pain but it makes her happy. The only place you can risk a sly fag at Hampstead Lycée is the footpath at the back of the school near the fence that separates Hampstead Lycée from Godspeed Boys' Academy. I'll admit, it does feel rather brave and decadent standing down there with a fag in your hand. If you DO get caught smoking it will become a matter of utmost GRIMNESS involving Mrs Prendergast 'the head', your house tutor, your parents, the local newsagent who sold you the packet of ten Silk Cut and even the local MP, Willam Dalmanger, (Conservative Party) if the poor git happens to be in his office and picks up the phone on the day the heinous incident occurs.

'Smoking kills!' Mrs Prendergast tells us once a week in assembly. 'And here at Hampstead Lycée I am educating the FUTURE LEADERS OF Great Britain! SO DYING WILL NOT BE TOLERATED!'

I always find the 'future leaders' part slightly hard to get my head around. Especially if I'm sitting next to girls like Olivia Brightwell who still has a full-time nanny called Mrs Tiggy who stands outside school at three-fifteen p.m. holding a peeled banana for her in case Olivia's sugar levels are low. Mrs Tiggy also puts Olivia's seatbelt on for her and even has wetwipes in her massive nanny handbag to take dinner smudges off Olivia's face. However when I asked Olivia last term what she did over the summer hols Olivia said her daddy had fixed her up with an internship at a government building in Whitehall in central London 'working with MI5 on matters of national security'. 'What do you mean!?' I said, and Olivia said she couldn't tell me as she'd 'signed an official secrets thingybobform, but it was to do with listening in on phonecalls to help on this war we're having against Muslims'. I told Olivia we weren't at war with the Muslims but her eyes glazed over then so I decided to shut up. 'Daddy says I'm terribly good at noticing stuff,' she said to me. 'He says I could be the head of MI5!' I'm glad no one at Hampstead Lycée thinks I'm remotely clever as heaven knows what I'd end up in charge of.

'So, the weekend?' Striker coughed, sticking a Camel Lite in her gob and lighting up. Great clouds of filthy grey smoke began seeping from her nose and her mouth. Striker flapped her hand about, simply pushing the fumes in mine and Vixen's direction.

'Ugh, move, Striker, that smells like crap,' moaned Vixen.

'Oh calm down, Vix,' sighed Striker, 'it's a ciggie, not napalm.'

'This is an Angora wool Paul Smith scarf!' said Vixen. 'I feel beastly enough about the poor bunnies losing their fur without smelling like a crackhead's underpants too. I am so OVER you smoking already.'

'Oh for God's sake, I'll smoke over here then,' tutted Striker, moving five metres away, then waving at us dramatically. 'So, plans for the weekend!?'

'Oh my aunt's flying in from Mustique tonight,' said Vixen, 'so Frangipan and I said we'd go out to the house she's taking in Bath. We're going riding. I've not been out on a hack for yonks.'

'How jolly,' Striker said. 'Popz?'

'Oh don't know, really,' I said. 'Oh God . . . hang on . . . my new nephew is getting christened on Sunday. Uncle Augustus's baby with his wife, Isis? It's going to be in *Hello!* magazine, so Mother is going mental saying we all need to have our 'look' pre-agreed with her.'

Vixen and Striker both howled with laughter. They love it when my mother puts the Montague-Jones clan in *Hello!* magazine. They loved it especially when Mother was promoting her new Jocasta Montague-Jones Spa range and the whole family were photographed in matching peach towelling dressing-gowns wearing clay face masks beside a roaring log fire in a house that wasn't even ours. Striker still has a copy of it blu-takked onto her bedroom wall. She says it cheers her up every single day.

'OK, let's go shopping then!' Striker said. 'Here, hold this a moment.' Striker walked across to me and handed me the cigarette and got out her iPhone and started trying to find a website. 'Look at the new Vivienne Westwood body-con dresses on *net-a-porter*, aren't they amazing?'

'It's a christening, I'm not appearing on *Bootie-Quake Dance Off* on MTV Base.'

'True,' said Striker. 'Maybe something a touch softer.'

'Here, do you want this back?' I said, waving the stump of the stinky cigarette at her.

'Oh stub it out,' she said, 'it's nearly done.'

I trod on the cigarette butt, then chucked it through the fence onto the boys' side.

'Oh come on, Popz, let's have some fun! We haven't had fun since New Year's Eve. That was a lot of fun, wasn't it? Life should always be like that!' Striker said.

'Hmmm,' I said, remembering her grinding against Bizzle's knee to a song called 'Will You Be My Babydaddy?'

'I mean it, Popz! Let's go to Bond Street! Let's spend some bloody money. And we can go to the oyster bar on the fifth floor of House of Harvey afterwards and have champagne. I'll bring my fake ID. They'll serve anyone anyway.'

'Erm,' I said, 'I was thinking I'd just pop down to Agatha's Anthology in Hampstead High Street and buy something plain. And maybe a little fur shrug to jazz it up.'

'*Of course you were,*' Striker groaned, 'that's why it's a good job you've got me! I'm looking forward to tomorrow already! This week has been a massive fannyache. Let's let off some steam. I'll call for you at eleven and I'll have a car drop us in the West End. OK?'

'OK,' I said.

'Fantastiche!' Striker said. Something about the way she said that made me feel excited but also rather terrified.

SATURDAY 9TH JANUARY

I should trust my instincts. They rarely let me down. I could tell yesterday that Striker had a weird glint in her eye when she talked about going shopping. I KNEW we'd never get to bloody Bond Street and back without something occuring. The voice in my head warned me again when I jumped in the back of the Mercedes today and saw Striker sitting looking sublime but decidedly minxish in dark Dior sunglasses and a burgundy Moschino velour knee-length playsuit over tartan tights, with black high-heeled velvet court shoes with rows of diamonds up the heels. Striker looked like a villainess before she'd even opened her mouth. 'Morning!' she said. It was two o'clock by this point. This is 'morning' for Striker at the weekends.

'Good shoes,' I said. 'Are they Giuseppe Zanotti?'

I'd seen these shoes in my mother's new copy of *Vogue*, but I was wondering if they were high street copies as Striker's mother has been going mental recently about the money she spends.

'Exactly! Giuseppe Za-HOTTY more like,' said Striker. 'Net-a-porter delivered them by courier this morning. My mother is blowing her top. I'm getting my allowance cut off again, apparently.'

Striker doesn't take Paloma's threats seriously at all. To be quite honest, neither do I. Why should we? Striker gets away with murder. I heard my mother once say to Vixen's mother that she thinks Paloma is such a total pushover because Striker is an only child and Paloma had to struggle so hard to have her. Apparently Paloma had about four goes at that IVF test tube thingy that older women do to have babies when they can't get up the duff normally, and none of that worked, and in the end Paloma and her ex-husband, Striker's dad, went to Switzerland and paid about fifty thousand pounds in a top clinic and came back pregnant with Striker. Apparently Paloma was in church all the time when she was pregnant thanking God for this great gift. Mummy says it feels like that when you're pregnant. I'll take Mother's word for that. When Mummy was pregnant with Flash it seemed to me like there was a lot of weeing her knickers in Waitrose and plodding about like a baby hippopotamus.

Whatever, Paloma doesn't really stand up to Striker, and that was why she was sat next to me today wearing most of the Moschino autumn/winter collection and seven-hundred-quid shoes.

Meanwhile, I felt rather plain and lumpen in my flat, scuffed Gucci pumps and Top Shop dress. The thing is I've been dressing down more since I've been going out with Kwame. I don't like wearing things that make me look obviously like my daddy's got money, and I've put all my most ridiculously expensive jewellery that Granny has given me into the Montague-Jones safe behind the fridge downstairs in the kitchen.

And I've stopped wearing my Cartier watch. Kwame says that kids who walk about Hampstead wearing Cartier watches are practically advertising themselves to be mugged. Kwame says he's spoken to kids in his youth group who've mugged people and he says most of them think if someone looks rich then they can probably afford to lose the stuff they're taking anyway. Kwame says some kids reckon that as long as you don't hit the person too hard you've not really done them much harm anyway. Kwame says that's why some of muggers shake girls really hard until they give over their stuff as it doesn't leave any marks. Some muggers think that's being incredibly thoughtful. I was ruddy outraged when I heard this. 'What?' I squeaked. 'So almost giving someone post-traumatic stress disorder for YEARS as they thought they were about to be murdered is FINE as long as you don't leave bruises!'

'I don't think that!' Kwame said, 'I'm just telling you what kids have said to me. It's just road chat, innit?'

'Road chat? What's that?' I said.

'Stuff kids say on the road,' said Kwame.

'What road?!' I said, making a mental note to never go there.

'Not A road, THE road,' said Kwame. 'The road? The street? The ghetto? Whatever you want to call it.'

'Oh right,' I said, sighing, 'well these people sound charming. They should all be locked up permanently! If there's not enough prison places, we should put them on islands! Or prison boats!'

'It's a bit more complex than that, Poppet,' Kwame said to me.

'How?' I said.

'Well,' Kwame said, 'I think you need to ask why so many kids on the road end up like this? Y'know? Like, why has the Cottingham got so many young black kids with no money and no hope? And then two miles up the road there's Hampstead full of white kids with more money than they know what to do with. How do Hampstead kids all have three-thousand-quid watches in the first place?'

I winced when he said that. The whole 'white and black' thing. It's rather uncomfortable sometimes. OK, lots of times.

'I don't know!' I said. 'It doesn't mean people should get mugged though!'

'I know. I agree,' he said, giving me a kiss on the face, 'it's just that I've gotta try and understand this stuff. Fact is, Poppet, the only reason some of the kids speak to me at youth group is 'cos I don't go judging them. I just listen and tell them that in this life you can choose the way of the road or you can choose to live a good life. That's all I can do. Two choices. Make your mind up. And when I go off to university I don't even know who'll be here to tell them that.'

I was thinking about this conversation as Striker and I glided towards Bond Street on warmed leather seats in the back of a Merc. Striker was reading *Grazia*, showing me nine-hundred-pound Miu Miu handbags while simulaneously bashing out texts and emails to various people on her mother's staff telling them what she needed and didn't need and wanted and didn't want. Striker *did* want dinner at seven p.m. but she *didn't* want carbs. Striker *did* want her room re-painted in spring, but she *didn't* want her mother's interior designer to design it. That type of thing. At one point Striker's phone bleeped and she read a text that seemed to make her go rather wobbly. 'Gosh, he is so FORWARD,' she said.

'Who?!' I said.

'Oh I'm not telling you, yet,' she said, 'you'll just disapprove.'

'Fine,' I said, refusing to play her game. It's bound to be one of those rugby-obsessed idiots in Year thirteen at Godspeed that she occasionally gets tangled up with, despite our warnings.

'Jeremiah,' Striker said to the driver, 'we'll need you back outside Prada by about 4.30 p.m. Then we'll go over to House of Harvey as we're going for afternoon tea on the fifth floor.'

'No problem, miss,' said Jeremiah.

'Oh Popz, I've got my eye on this gorgeous batwing Prada dress.' said Striker, pointing at a fashion page. 'It's off the peg. Five hundred and fifty pounds. That's weirdly cheap really for Prada.'

'Mmm yeah,' I said. Suddenly I thought of Oceanspray, Shazzalla's mate, on the Cottingham Estate. Kwame told me yesterday that she had no electricity for two days last week as she was too proud to ask anyone to loan her ten pounds. Her and her little boy had just sat in the dark eating cold soup out of a tin until Shazzalla's mother found her. Sometimes I almost resent Kwame Kobina for bringing these people with their awful bad fortune into my world. It's like a door's been opened and now I can't stop reality barging its way in all the time going HELLO, HELLO, HELLO, WON'T YOU THINK ABOUT THIS FOR A WHILE, POPPET?

'Popz, y'know what you'd look INCREDIBLE in tomorrow?' said Striker, 'A little black Prada skirt and jacket and a pair of these Oscar de la Renta heels. Look at these purple-lilacy flowery ones here?'

I glanced at the page. My heart felt mushy at first sight. I don't really get all dippy about shoes much, I'm not that type of girl at all, but these shoes were GORGEOUS. Not just shoes, more like portable art-installations. Delicate lilac wool woven into a pointy slipper with ties that criss-cross up the ankles and a delicate three-inch silver heel.

'Oh my word, they ARE beautiful!' I said, grabbing the magazine off her. 'Oh. They're eight hundred and forty pounds? That seems a lot of money.'

'Poppet,' said Striker, 'they're by Oscar de la Renta.

They need to be a lot of money or everyone would be wearing them, then they'd not be special at all. That's the point.'

'I suppose,' I said.

Sometimes you can't argue with Striker's logic.

The next few hours were a blur of shoes, frocks and frilly things. Striker whisked me into Bodwin's Boutique on Bond Street where lots of A-list stars go as they stock lots of designer stuff. The security guard on the door looked us up and down casually then chivvied us past with a friendly 'Good afternoon, ladies!' leaving a bunch of tourists in damp raincoats standing outside with their mouths agog and their noses against the glass doors. Striker says the staff in places like Prada, Gucci or Bodwin's can tell immediately that we come from money simply by the way we walk and our bone structure and the way our skin glows with health like we've never eaten anything with trans-fat in it in our lives. I hate it when she says that, even if I think she possibly has a point. Everyone at Hampstead Lycée does have a certain look about them. We've got no tattoos, no multiple piercings and no one is obese at all. I mean, obviously we've got plenty of self-harmers, anorexics and depressives, but they tend to keep that all hidden under their pure silk Hampstead Lycée school blouses. Outwardly, we all look pretty serene and refined.

As Striker headed straight to the day-dress section to

find me my perfect *Hello!* christening outfit, I looked behind me where the security guard now seemed to be arguing with a young girl at the door. She was about twenty-seven, black, dressed neatly in a black raincoat with a tied waist and long black boots. The girl was very angry indeed.

'What do you mean *valued customers only*?' she was saying. 'I'm arrksk-sking you politely! I need to buy my niece a Prada keyring for her birthday.' The girl said 'ask' like Shazzalla says it. With an extra 'k'. I always laugh when Shazzalla says this, and she says, 'Shattit, posho,' and takes the mickey out of me for saying, 'Wow, super!' But the atmosphere wasn't funny now at all.

'Well I'm ASKING you to understand,' said the guard, 'that the shop is full at the moment! You'll need to come back later. We've only got limited security on today.'

'Hang on? Limited security,' the woman said, 'there's only about six customers in there anyway!'

'Come back later,' the man said, shutting the door and locking it. I felt really bad for her.

'Bloody keyrings,' said the security guy, walking back past one of the sales assistants, who was staring into space as she had literally nothing to do.

'Tsk, I know,' tutted the girl.

I felt angry. I wanted to say something but I didn't want to cause a scene.

'Poppet!' Striker shouted. 'OK, try this skirt and this

blouse with this shruggy-shawl thing,' she said, passing me an armful of clothes, 'and I'm going to try this dress.' Striker waved the batwing dress from the magazine. 'Hello, can we have some help?' she shouted at the sales assistant, who jumped to life suddenly, plastering a big smile across her face like our best friend meeting us from the Arrivals gate at Heathrow after a world trip.

'No problem!' she smiled, scooping the clothes out of our arms. 'Why don't I pop all of these items into the cublicle for you?' she said, 'then you won't get weighed down as you're browsing. Are you after anything in particular, so I can help you?'

'It's for my friend really,' Striker said, pointing at me. 'She has a rather smart christening at Westminster Abbey.'

'I see,' said the assistant. 'OK, well with your colouring I'm thinking dark greys, midnight blues, pale creams?'

She was absolutely right. I love these colours. The assistant was being so nice. I wish I'd not seen her tutting about the girl who wanted a keyring.

'Can I get you two ladies a drink of something? A glass of champagne?'

'That would be *wonderful*,' Striker said quickly before the assistant worked out how old we were. She disappeared and Striker and I started trying on our clothes. The champagne arrived on a silver tray and we started getting giggly, then two other assistants arrived with armfuls of knitwear, day-dresses, shoes and quite formal gowns that were far too old for us but we tried on anyway as after half a glass of champagne we already felt slightly tipsy.

Eventually Striker clicked her fingers and said, 'OK, Poppet, I love this skirt, this blouse and this jacket.'

The assistant nodded solemly as if our fashion taste was exquisite, then she took them away and wrapped them in several metres of soft pale-green tissue paper and then popped them into a crisp black Bodwin's Boutique bag.

'That will be three thousand four hundred and fifty-six pounds please. How will you be paying?' she said.

'Oh,' I said, getting out my black Amex card, 'here.'

I don't recall feeling particularly guilty about this. I was quite giddy as Striker had been making me laugh so much. Plus, I've seen Mummy and Kitten spend much more than this. Mummy often spends four and a half grand on one Valentino dress for one red carpet awards ceremony.

The assistant swiped my card, placed the receipt into a pretty green envelope and handed it to me, and then the security guard walked us to the door and made sure we got to our car.

It was when we'd finally got to the fifth floor of House of Harvey and were sipping Kir Royale cocktails and eating calamari that Striker finally piped up, 'And the best bit of all about today, Poppet, is the enormous discount we got at Bodwin's!'

'What do you mean?' I laughed. 'I paid full price for everything!'

'Oh you're forgetting the little extras they popped in for free!' She smiled, naughtily.

'Like what?' I said, being as ever enormously slow on the uptake.

Striker leaned forwards and unbuttoned the front of her velour playsuit, which, now I looked closer, seemed to be bulging at the buttonholes slightly as if she'd eaten too much pudding over Christmas. Underneath the playsuit was the black batwing Prada dress with the pricetag still on.

Striker had stolen it.

I felt my blood run very very cold.

'OH MY GOD, STRIKER,' I said, my head swivelling around frantically to see if anyone was watching us. I almost expected to see that security guard closing in on us, accompanied by police officers. 'Tell me you didn't steal that bloody dress?!' I snapped, 'THERE'S CCTV CAMERAS ALL OVER THAT SHOP. Striker, what the hell are you doing?'

'They'll never suspect it was us!' howled Striker. 'We spent well over three thousand pounds in that bloody shop. We're so rich we don't NEED to steal anything.'

'So why did you do it?!' I hissed. My face was the shade of a postbox by now, I'm certain.

'Pghghghg . . . oh I don't know. It's a buzz, isn't it?' Striker said. 'In fact, that's the biggest buzz I've had so far this year. You have to try it. It really makes your heart go crazy! A bit like power-plate at the gym!'

'I ruddy will not!' I said. 'Striker, this is preposterous. You're an idiot. I'm . . . I'm!'

'You're really boring,' tutted Striker. 'Jesus, Poppet, how old are you? Sixteen or sixty? Oh cheer up and drink your Kir Royale. It's Saturday.'

I closed my mouth and fumed silently while Striker sat examining a new iPhone app. She didn't seem remotely bothered. After about a minute I gathered my thoughts together and gave her a little smile to say I didn't want to fight. Yes, I know I should have said more but I didn't want to be the sensible one always spoiling the fun. Even if I was thinking to myself that stealing a dress from a shop is probably exactly the same as stealing a handbag from a person in the street. It's still stealing. It's still taking something that's not yours just because you think you can. It doesn't matter if you're doing it in Bodwin's or down the Cottingham Estate, you're still a thief. At least some of the people down the Cottingham Estate were literally skint and starving and had some sort of excuse.

MONDAY 11TH JANUARY

Flash didn't get terribly good feedback about that Art homework I did for him.

'In fairness, Poo-Pop, it looked nothing like Humpty Dumpty!' he said to me this morning. We were in the kitchen eating toast together, laughing at Kitten in the garden doing Astanga Yoga. Every time she bent over for a difficult position, our dog Macbeth would come over and sniff her bum. It was more hilarious than anything on TV that's meant to be funny.

'Excuse me, what do you mean, it didn't look like Humpty Dumpty?' I said to Flash. 'It was a ruddy egg man, made of crushed eggshells, sitting on a wall. Who else was it?'

Flash tutted at me and carried on feeding Dragon his baby porridge. 'It looked more like that man who lives in that bar in EastEnders,' he said, 'the one who is always shouting.'

'Phil Mitchell?' I said. 'No it didn't! Pgghh, it was Year Three Art. I wasn't doing the fine artwork on the ruddy Sistine Chapel.'

'*Thankfully*,' said Flash, handing me my Maths exercise book open at a page of complex logarithms.

'Was it very hard?' I sighed. 'I'm totally lost with it now.'

'Quite hard,' Flash said. 'I mean, we used to do much harder stuff at Junior Mensa.' His little face looked sad.

'Oh,' I said.

Mummy has been asked not to bring Flash back to Junior Mensa until he agrees to respect other children's views, particularly on topics such as religion and evolution, and stop being a disruption.

Apparently Flash was warned before Christmas to

STOP laughing at a little girl called Guinevere when she mentioned things like Noah's ark and how God created the world in seven days.

Apparently Flash called her a 'blithering God-bothering idiot'.

'But she IS, Poppet!' Flash said to me again this morning. 'In fact, how can Guinevere even BE in Junior Mensa when she thinks the world is here because God saved all the animals on a big ship! That's just MENTAL. The world is here because of SCIENCE!'

I didn't know what to say. It was seven-fifteen in the morning, which felt pretty early to be doing whether God exists, although I was jolly certain he must do or why would places like Westminster Abbey still be allowed to exist in the London WC1 postcode, which is prime real estate land? Surely they'd have turned it into luxury apartments?

'Well whatever, Flash,' I said, finishing my pomegranate juice. 'You can't just go around calling people stupid. That's why you got banned.'

'But they are all stupid,' mumbled Flash. 'All that praying people do, Poppet. It's just people talking to no one.'

I didn't know what to say. I sometimes pray. I sometimes find myself basically pleading with God to help me out of stuff, like he's one of the X-Men really who can sort out all the messes I get into.

'Well even if he doesn't exist,' I said to Flash, packing

pens into his book bag, 'maybe some people just need imaginary friends. Like when you had Crispin the Space Pirate.'

Flash gave me one of his death glares.

'Crispin the Space Pirate wasn't an imaginary friend, Poppet,' he said. 'He was real. He just kept disappearing because he didn't want to meet you.'

'Oh, yes,' I said. 'Yes, that's right.'

Just then Kitten breezed into the kitchen carrying a yoga mat, wearing bum-skimming neon-pink shorts and a white string vest. Kitten was pulling that demented 'I'm so zen' face she does after long Astanga sessions that have sent oxygen to parts of her brain that certainly weren't being accessed when she lived nocturnally in nightclubs fuelled solely on vodka and Red Bull.

'Kitten, when is Mummy coming home?' Flash asked. 'I can't access her online iCalendar.'

'Mmm . . . about four days' time, I think,' Kitten replied. 'Mummy is staying in Valencia until she can convince a farmer to sell all of his antique milking stools. She wants to ship them home and use them as manicurist's seats in the health spa that Aunty Pearl is opening.'

'Won't they smell of old milk and cow poo?' said Flash.

'Probably,' said Kitten, distractedly. 'She'll get the work experience kids to give them a good scrub though. Anyway, look, shouldn't you two be out of the door for school? I won't have you both being late. Come on, hurry up!'

Well I nearly choked when she said that.

'You're NOT my mother, Kitten,' I sighed. 'And at my age you were thrown out of school for skiving off! You got paparazzied in Soho House with the lead singer of the Blank-Faced Babies. You'd told him you were twenty! You were on pages three and four of the *News of the World*!'

Kitten didn't even flinch.

'What a good memory you have, Poppet,' she said, smiling warmly. 'Anyway for your information, while Mummy and Daddy are away and Knute is still chained to that bulldozer near Heathrow airport, I'm the oldest here and I'm in charge. So in a weird way, I AM YOUR MOTHER. GO TO SCHOOL!'

'Pah!' I snorted. 'Whatever.'

'Oh, and whilst I remember,' Kitten said. 'Whatever you're doing on Wednesday evening, cancel it, we're having an African Heritage session with Dragon. We're going to remind him of his cultural roots.'

'What? Oh God, really?' I gasped. I didn't actually think we were going to have to do this.

'Yes! It's going to be AWESOME!' she said. 'I'll find some recipes online today! I'm working on our costumes!'

'Our what?'

Kitten isn't my mother, she's actually WORSE than my mother 'cos at least Mummy flies out of the country and leaves me alone sometimes.

'Kitten,' I said as I was putting on my coat, 'have you

got any holidays booked or anything?'

'Oh, crikey, NO!' she said. 'My counsellor at Paradise Vision Rehab Centre said that it's enormously important I reconnect with my family after losing so many years to my inner demons. I'm staying here.'

'Oh wonderful,' I said, trudging slowly towards the front door.

WEDNESDAY 13TH JANUARY

'Kitten, that's not what I think it is, is it?' I said tonight as I arrived home from my sculpting class to spot a bag of blood and body bits chopped up on the kitchen worksurface. 'Please, say it's not.'

'Oh don't be so squeamish, said Kitten, hacking at a sweet potato with Mrs Minsk's best peeler. '*Everyone* eats it in Africa.'

'I know but . . . well, I like goats,' I said. 'To look at I mean. Not to eat. Granny's friend, Lady Margoyles, used to keep them in her orchards – do you remember them? They used to run up and nuzzle our hands. Goats are rather friendly.'

'Yes, I do remember,' said Kitten, looking quite guilty. 'Well, I made Mrs Minsk buy it from the Halal butcher in Kilburn, so at least it had a holy death. Well it did if it was a Muslim goat. Bit of a bummer for it if it was an agnostic.'

'Oh gngngn,' I muttered, feeling rather queasy.

I hate thinking about where meat comes from. I don't like to imagine my rack of lamb with a face, frolicking about enjoying the sun, thinking, 'Oh what shall I do today?' then, 'Baaa. Oh look, a man in a van is coming to get us,' THWACK. I'm beginning to agree with Cordelia Grossop, the emo in my class, that meat may very well be murder. I really wish murder wasn't so damn delicious slow roasted with garlic and rosemary and served with potatoes dauphinoise.

As Kitten hacked away at dinner, little Dragon sat close by in his highchair, his DVD player open in front of him, watching a Baby Einstein video.

'Hello, Dragon, are you happy?' I said.

Now that he's nearly two, we can ask him little questions and he's starting to understand us, which is supercool.

Dragon thought for a while, placing his hand to his chin while he was pondering just like Flash does. Dragon copies the things we do a lot. The pondering face is so cute that if you measured it on a cute-o-meter it would melt.

'Yess'appy,' Dragon said.

'See, Kitten? Dragon's happy!' I said. 'We don't need to make the goat curry. I don't care what bloody Mrs Demansk the social worker thinks.'

Kitten pretended to be deaf.

'Anyway, can toddlers eat spicy food?' I said.

'The curry is for us, not him,' said Kitten. 'Dragon is

having mashed sweet potato. I thought we could get him to grow accustomed to the smells. And the, um, general, African ambience.'

'Oh,' I said, then I decided to shut up. The truth was, I've never seen Kitten attempt anything more complex in the kitchen than spicy chicken Supernoodles with salad cream on toast. This foray into West African cuisine was unnerving me. At the same time I could see Kitten was doing this for the good of us all. She's tired of social workers giving mean statements to journalists about Dragon not understanding his culture. Kitten has started doing things 'for the good of us all'.

Wow. Mummy certainly got her money's worth out of rehab with Kitten.

'Oh bloody hell.' Kitten frowned, staring at the cut on her hand where she'd hacked herself with the scraper.

'You OK?' I said.

'Yes,' she lied.

'Do you want an elastoplast for that?' I said. 'Or are you going to bleed all over the kitchen?'

Kitten was staring at her hand. She looked rather demoralized.

'Actually, drop some in the curry, it might take our minds off the ruddy taste.'

Kitten narrowed her eyes at me. 'Well, I was thinking you could do with some iron,' she said. 'I mean, by the look of your skin you're clearly perilously anaemic.'

'Pah! How rude!' I gasped, feigning deep offence.

'Actually, here have a suck,' smiled Kitten, wickedly waving her hand at me. 'It might make your boobs grow!'

'Oh you've crossed a line now,' I said, gasping. 'You absolute cow!'

Kitten's little joke had cheered her up immensely. She was giggling to herself.

'I don't care about my tits, ACTUALLY,' I said. 'At least these "perfect rosebuds", as *Grazia* magazine calls them, will still be facing in the right direction when I'm thirty! Unlike your big wobbling kachongs, which will be down by your knees!'

'Oh really?!' laughed Kitten.

'Ughghghghghow!' frowned Flash, sat at the kitchen table, putting both hands over his ears. 'Stop talking about your boobs! It's DISGUSTING.'

'Sorry, Flash,' we laughed.

'And I'm hunnnnngggry,' whined Flash, 'I don't want the dead goat, can't we order takeaway?'

I looked at my big sister hopefully.

'Oh ruddy hell . . . OK,' said Kitten. 'But it needs to be something African! THIS IS AFRICAN NIGHT! Hey Flash, phone Cyril and ask what he would choose. And we're definitely still doing the dresses. Aren't we, Popz?'

'Of course we are,' I said.

We ran up the spiral staircase to my bedroom, which ever since I fell in love with Kwame had been turning into a post-apocalyptic vision of shoes, muddy sports socks, a pile of damp towels with Macbeth the labrador snoring in the middle of them, half-full coffee cups and untouched GCSE coursework. I really should tidy it up. Definitely at some point this month. I'm growing quite used to the mess though. Plus, one of the mugs has amazing mould growing in it and the other day I SWORE I could almost make out the face of Jesus in the spores. It's a holy mug! I'm rather psyched that my bedroom might turn out to be a great celebrated religious shrine like Lourdes where people bring their sick to be healed. I told Striker this the other day and she accused me of experimenting with my mother's back pain relief pharmaceuticals again.

'Are these the dresses Mummy brought us back from Liberia last year?' I said, picking up a long emerald-green creation I was sure we'd given to Mrs Minsk to use as dusters.

'Yes, she didn't rip them up!' said Kitten. 'She said she thought we were being silly girls and we'd want them some day.'

'Holy hell,' I said, 'that woman can read us like a book.'

'Damn straight,' Kitten said, picking up her Liberian dress and flinging off T-shirt and leggings. She had nothing on underneath. 'Right, don't mind me!'

'Ugh, God,' I groaned, 'too much va-jay-jay! My eyes!'

Kitten has a very lackadaisical approach to nudity. Kitten thinks nothing of holding a conversation while sitting on the loo with no bra on, or striding about the house with her front carriage on show like it's part of the

Turner Modern Art exhibition. Small wonder our window cleaner spends hours on end polishing her bedroom window with his tongue lolling out and one hand mysteriously in his pocket. YUK.

'Jesus, these things aren't exactly flattering, are they?' Kitten said, looking in the mirror. 'How does anyone ever get snogged in Liberia?'

As she span and preened, I plonked down on the bed picking a copy of the *Evening Standard* newspaper out of my schoolbag.

'Oh crikey, what's Frankie Walcott been up to now?' sighed Kitten, spotting the front page headline.

'He punched a policeman outside the Farenheit Club,' I said.

'Noooooooo!' said Kitten.

I've not seen Frankie, or His Royal Highness Prince Francis, for ages.

I used to bump into him at tea-parties a lot when I was about seven, but these days it's not often as we're in totally different groups. Frankie is the Queen's youngest grandson, but the Queen has lots of children so Frankie is about twelfth in line to the throne. It's still lots higher up than Kitten and myself, obviously, as we're up in the eightieth to a hundredth bracket, but let's face it, it would take a pretty big Al-Qaeda explosion to leave Frankie, Poppet or myself wearing the crown going, 'HELLO, CITIZENS, I AM YOUR LEADER'. I pity Great Britain if ever I was in charge.

'More details, please!' said Kitten.

'OK, well he was in Farenheit apparently,' I said, scanning the story. 'Which he wasn't meant to be as he's still seventeen, but security guards claimed he wasn't drinking. However, now a source at the the Farenheit Club has produced the bar receipt for his booth and there's six bottles of vodka on it.'

'Oh God, they'll serve anyone at the Farenheit Club,' tutted Kitten. 'I was dancing on the bar in my bra there by the time I was fifteen.' A tiny naughty twinkle flashed across Kitten's face before she remembered to tell herself lewd drunkeness was nothing to be proud of.

'So, apparently Frankie left at four a.m.,' I said. 'And a fight broke out with the paparazzi. And somehow a policeman got punched. It says Buckingham Palace are expected to "react with the utmost fury".'

'Pah!' laughed Kitten. 'That bunch of toothless old farts. What will they do to him? Cut off usage of the royal bloody helicopter?'

'It says here,' I said, pretending to read the newspaper. 'He's had his bare bum smacked by the Queen and he's been told he doesn't own Dorset any more.'

Well Kitten nearly wet her non-existent knickers at that. 'When did you start being so funny?' she said, wiping her eyes.

'I've *always* been funny!' I said. 'You just stopped finding me funny when you started being a knobhead and taking drugs.'

'True,' sighed Kitten. 'I'm sorry about that.'

'It's OK,' I said.

We sat in silence for a little while.

I stared at the photo of Frankie. He was definitely much taller and slimmer than the last time I'd seen him. He certainly didn't possess cheekbones then. Frankie was always a little ball of flesh on feet, to be honest.

'"Tutors have expressed concerns about the Prince's increasingly unruly behaviour and have doubts about him completing his A-levels . . ."' groaned Kitten, reading out from the paper. 'Pghghghg! As IF any of the Walcotts could get an A-level! They're the most in-bred family in town! Princess Jocelyn did all her GCSEs THREE TIMES and still only got one "C" in Nutrition and that's very ironic as she's as big as a Shire horse! And whenever she loses any weight she calls up the paps to take pictures of her on the beach in Mustique in a bikini and says, "I've lost all the weight living on fresh papaya" AND YOU CAN SEE THE LIPOSUCTION HOLES on her bum!'

Kitten was being a terrible bitch but it was funny. She's always hilarious when she starts ranting about the A-list Buckingham Palace royals. We've always found them *très amusant*. They'd show up to birthday tea-parties when we were all tiny, Prince Frankie dressed like a mini naval officer in a navy blazer and deckshoes and his big sisters Princess Jocelyn and Princess Margot in scarlet velour dresses with white lace collars, and knee-length white socks with black buckled shoes. Margot was always boo-hooing about nothing and her nanny was forever taking her somewhere quiet to cuddle her. OK, when I say 'boo-hooing about nothing', at one tea-party at Clarence House Kitten tied Margot's plaits to a door handle then banged the door really hard. This made Margot cry till she sicked up trifle down her nostrils. The Montague-Jones children didn't get invited back to any of the more exclusive palace parties after that. Mummy wasn't really so bothered. She just sighed and said she was rather glad to be left out of the loop with the A list as they were a bunch of cripplingly out-of-touch freaks anyway.

'They need to step hard on Frankie,' said Kitten. 'Or he'll end up ruining his life.'

'Hmmm,' I said, pulling the dress over my head, hoping Kitten wasn't slipping into one of her holier-than-thou rants.

'Oh amazing!' giggled Kitten, beholding me in my floor-length emerald ensemble. 'Do you think Dragon will even notice?'

'Kitten,' I said, 'we're both enormous and green. We look like mutant courgettes. Of course he will.'

We stepped carefully downstairs holding hands, picking up our dresses just like we did years ago when we'd ransack Mummy's wardrobe for her dresses then prance about pretending to be fairy-goddesses arriving at a very special ball.

'Are you ready?' said Kitten, grabbing hold of my hand as she turned the knob on the kitchen door.

'Yes,' I said.

'Helllllooooo Dragon!' we both shouted.

Dragon looked up from his DVD, his eyes widened and a very odd expression flashed across his face, first it was almost a smile, but then he threw back his head, opened his mouth so all of his back teeth were showing and he SCREEEEEEAMED. In fact he screamed so loudly he woke the au pair who was sleeping off a hangover upstairs in his nursery.

'Oh Dragon, come here!' cried Kitten. 'It's us! It's your sisters! Look, it's Kitten and . . . Oh, this is a complete disaster!'

But the ironic thing was, it wasn't a disaster, because once Dragon calmed down and started laughing again, we listened to Liberian music, and the pizza Flash ordered arrived (a Caribbean Hot with Jerk Chicken, which wasn't African at all but that's what Cyril told Flash he would choose). It was just Kitten, Flash, Dragon and myself sitting around the dining table being silly and chatting. Not a disaster at all. In fact one of the nicest nights that has ever happened in 1 Octavia Square for a long time. We were hanging out. Just like a normal family.

It was almost too good to be true.

THURSDAY 28TH JANUARY

Holy hell. What a hideous day. My *jour de terribleness* began thus: I was woken from a delicious snooze at seven-thirty a.m. by Flash crouching by my bed, poking my forehead, saying, 'Poppet? Poppet? Mummy says you have to answer your phone. She's flipping out about something. Have you been naughty again, Poppet? What have you done?'

I opened one eye and tried batting him away like a wasp.

'Stop poking me, Flash! No I haven't been naughty,' I said, meanwhile frantically trying to think what I was most likely to have been caught for.

The New Year's Eve party lie?

The holy shrine of Jesus mould mug?

Encouraging Flash's Montague-Jones family tree project, which had led him to telephone Granny, basically accusing her of emerald theft and grand-scale fraud? It could have been any of these things.

'How angry does Mummy sound?' I said.

Flash pondered for a moment.

'Well, not as angry as when I smashed the Russian chandelier with the cricket ball . . . more like when Knute left the poo on Downing Street.'

'Hmmm,' I said, 'chuck me my iPhone, it's under that towel.'

Flash did this without quibbling. He adores a bit of family drama, he loves to be centre-stage thrusting his tiny oar in. There were four missed calls from Mother, plus a text message that read:

HAMPSTEAD LYCEE. 2.15 P.M. SEE YOU THERE. I CAN THINK OF BETTER WAYS TO SPEND AN AFTERNOON, POPPET. MUMMY.

As I peered at the screen, the phone began ringing. I answered to hear a totally irate Striker.

'Has your mother had an email from Prendergast too?' she shouted.

'OH GOD, yes, I think so,' I said. My stomach was starting to catch up with my brain now. I leaped up and ran towards the bathroom and took the rest of Striker's phonecall on the loo.

'Those bloody pigs,' Striker ranted. 'What did yours say?'

'I don't know what mine said,' I said, 'I've just found out. My mother's been called into the school though.'

'Mine says Mrs Prendergast wants to urgently discuss my grave behavioural issues,' said Striker. 'Pah! What is wrong with our behaviour!?'

'OUR behaviour?' I spluttered. You're the one who smokes fags, dyes your hair and flashes your knickers at the gardener. Why have I got an email? Has Vixen's dad got an email?'

'Nooooooo,' roared Striker, 'of course not. Vixen is Little Miss Clean-Knickers, as ruddy ever. Oh, God, gotta go, I'm locking myself in the library until Mother goes to work so she can't start nagging me.'

The line went dead.

I called my mother's phone but it went to a voicemail message saying she'd be on a plane for the next few hours. This meant she was flying back from Valencia. I hoped to God it wasn't just for the meeting. This was getting serious.

I called again and left a message in my best pathetic, confused little-girl-lost voice claiming not to have a clue what this was all about.

Then I called Kwame, hoping for sympathy and reassurance, but the moment I told him about the letter he started being quite frosty.

'Poppet, you said you were studying for those GCSEs,' he whispered as he was using his phone in the British Library, where he was doing extra research for one of his projects like the ginormous goody-two-shoes that he is. 'You're getting letters home in Year Eleven? Poppet, I've got kids coming down to my youth group with tags on their legs with more focus than you right now.'

Well this made me really jolly irate.

'Kwame,' I snapped, 'you've got kids at your youth group who've stuck knives at businessmen's throats at Kilburn Overground Station and stolen their shoes. Don't compare me to them, THANK YOU VERY MUCH.'

Then I put the phone down abruptly. I love him, I'm pretty sure I do, but he gets on my nerves sometimes. It's always: 'Oh you don't understand me, you don't understand where I'm coming from.' Well he doesn't understand me at all.

* * *

The morning slouched by MEGA SLOWLY. Striker had made the idiotic error of bragging about our behavioural emails to the girls in our class during home period, so now everyone was gossiping about about it and LOVING the sense of intrigue – none more so than Blitzen Trapper, who I'm beginning to think may actually be possessed by a Satanic force as she only expresses true pleasure when she's involved in acts of malicious cruelty.

'Well *bon voyage*, Poppet!' Blitzen purred in Biology, tossing about her platinum-blonde bob cut. 'This may be your last afternoon at Lycée! They're bound to expel you! Bye bye!' Blitzen waved her tiny hand, waggling the delicate fingers all tipped with dark-red nail varnish.

'Shut up, Blitzen,' I snapped at her. 'I've not done anything.'

I've started standing my ground a bit more with Blitzen these days. Kwame says peaceful protest is the best way to tackle bullies, like that man Ghandi who wore the giant nappy in the olden days used to believe. I know Kwame is right and violence is never the solution to things, although with Blitzen I do find myself thinking how satisfying a roundhouse slap that loosens all her new Da Vinci tooth veneers might sound.

'Byeeeeeesybyebye, Poppet!' hooted Belle Caribou and Amelia Strang, Blitzen's best friends, who were sitting beside her.

'COULD YOU GIRLS PLEASE CONCENTRATE ON

THE TEXTBOOK IN FRONT OF YOU?' shouted Mr Abdul, who'd told us off several times already this lesson.

'Oh let's stop,' whispered Belle pitifully, as if I was a puppy they were kicking for pleasure. 'It's terrifying really. Poppet will probably be rattling on the gates of Thamesmoor Park Comprehensive by this afternoon, begging to join all the Cottingham chavs and ghetto-fodder!'

'HAHAHAHAHAHAHA!' Blitzen howled, which quickly spread through her demonic amigos like the plague.

'HAHAHAHAHHAHAHAHHAHA!' all three of them cackled.

Seriously, I would NEVER have taken Biology if I'd known I'd end up sharing a bench with these three witches.

'Oh my gosh, Thamesmoor Park Comp, like, SHUDDER,' said Amelia. 'Daddy had to go there a few weeks ago. He was having his photo taken outside the gates for the new Conservative Party manifesto. Daddy told me it was like "spot the white man" over there. There were hardly any white pupils. Everyone is brown. Like Pakistani, or black, or like, y'know, whatever. Not white anyway.'

'Oh I know!' said Blitzen. 'I'm so glad we're here. I mean, I'm not racist at all, in fact, I've just given Alitash my last tampon in the loos and she's from Ethiopia, but I just would rather, y'know, be with people who look like us. I feel much safer here.'

'That IS racist actually,' I said, staring at my textbook.

Blitzen looked outraged. 'No it's NOT!' she said.

'It is.' I said, 'being scared of anyone who isn't white and not wanting them in our school is racist.'

'It's NOT racist,' she said. 'But DO EXCUSE ME, POPPET, we know you're very keen on promoting race relations.'

I thought she was meaning Dragon, but there was something more sneaky in her tone of voice.

'What's that supposed to mean?' I said.

'Nothing,' Blitzen said. 'I'm just saying, you're quite the opposite of prejudice towards black boys – sorry, black people – aren't you?'

I glared at her, thinking: Do you know about Kwame? She smiled back. I sat at my desk FUMING.

So here I was on the day my mother was being called into Lycée, shortly after slamming the phone down on my boyfriend and then picking a fight with Blitzen Trapper about racial politics. I am quite literally a solid-gold nutter. The only way I could possibly make life more uncomfortable for myself was if I popped over to Godspeed Boys' Academy and scampered topless about the classrooms asking randoms whether they thought I was developing an inverted left nipple.

By lunchtime my brain was melting. In the lunch hall I couldn't manage a morsel of food, even when Vixen buttered a soft bread roll for me, spread it with Philadelphia cheese, then tried to feed me small pieces like she was hand-rearing a sickly baby crow.

Meanwhile, Striker demolished an enormous bowl of French fries covered in ketchup and mayonnaise. 'Well I hope they do bloody throw me out,' she said casually between chomps. 'All the best people were expelled from school or college. Like . . . like Nancy Spungen. That woman who went out with Sid Vicious from the Sex Pistols in the 70s. She had great style, didn't she?'

'Yes, I watched that film with you, Striker,' I said. 'She ended up as a heroin addict and then Sid stabbed her to death.'

'And Barbarella Bang from the Awful Sparks!' Striker said, ignoring me. 'She was expelled from school when she was fourteen for arson, wasn't she? I love her, she's amazing.'

'She's been in a mental hospital for over a decade,' I said. 'Call me boring, but I don't want to be in the same category as stabbed-to-death-lady and an inside-a-padded-cell-girl. I'd rather not be expelled at all.'

Striker shrugged. Sometimes I think she finds me rather square, which is fine as sometimes I find her rather annoying.

'OK, well, showtime,' she said, waltzing off for her one-fifteen appointment.

'It'll be fine,' said Vixen, rubbing my hand. 'Don't worry, you've not done anything. Have you?'

It was starting to dawn on me that this was the problem. I hadn't done anything. I'd barely moved a muscle at school since Christmas. My coursework was late, I'd barely done any homework, I'd even skived school a few days and stayed in bed playing Doodlejump on my iPhone instead of turning up for cross-country running. But what EXACTLY, pray tell, is the point of cross-country running? I'm one hundred per cent sure there is nowhere 'cross country' I'd ever desire to be so desperately that I'd go on foot in the rain wearing small gym-knickers with an angry lesbian in a tracksuit shouting in my ear. If they want me to take this school seriously then they need to stop making bits of it such a JOKE.

As I walked upstairs to the school administration centre I caught sight of Mummy standing in reception. I recognized her immediately by the way she stands – confidently, with her shoulders pulled back. Mummy is always nagging me do something about my posture. 'Stop walking with hunched shoulders like you're constantly apologizing,' she always says. So I pulled my shoulders back and tried to walk like I had nary a care in the world.

'Hi, Mummy,' I said.

'Hello, darling,' she said. She looked rather scary and business-like in a long leather Donna Karan belted trench coat and Jimmy Choo shoes. 'Why am I here? What have you done?'

Mummy's face was incredibly calm and kind. I realize

now this was due to the fresh Botox she had put in just after New Year, when she spent a lot of the first week in January bleeding with a forehead all puckered like an alien from *Battlestar Galactica*, but right then I mistook it for genuine sympathy. In fact, right then I felt like falling to her feet and confessing EVERYTHING about the shoplifting on Bond Street and the New Year's Eve party with Bizzle with the tag on his leg for cocaine dealing.

Thankfully, just that second, the door to Mrs Prendergast's office swung open and out of it fell Paloma Earhart and Striker. It's safe to say Striker appeared to have lost a lot of her blaséness about the situation. 'It's a load of BLOODY LIES!!' She was squawking. 'I didn't buy my GCSE coursework off anyone! And I don't smoke either! Those photographs had been photoshopped! And as for everything else on your stupid list . . .'

'Jocasta,' Paloma greeted Mummy.

'Hello, Paloma,' Mummy said.

'You're PATHETIC, all of you,' went on Striker, jabbing a finger at Prendergast and then all of us, myself included, but in truth she was so worked up I don't think she'd even seen me and my mother. 'It's PATHETIC you have the time to concoct these stories and stitch me up.'

'Be quiet, Striker,' said Paloma. 'Mrs Prendergast, I must apologize again for my daughter. Striker is experiencing anger issues since her father re-married and their relationship broke down. Striker's identity as a young adult has been jarred severely since her father withdrew emotionally and created a life with his girlfriend and son.'

I cringed HARD when Paloma said that. Striker doesn't like talking about her father. We've been avoiding the subject for the past few months.

There was a horrible silence, then Striker said loudly, 'Why don't you both stop psycho-analysing me! You're the mental ones. Especially you, you twisted old goat!'

Mrs Prendergast's face didn't even flicker. That's the problem with shouting a lot, after a while people stop taking you remotely seriously.

Striker stormed through the swing doors and vanished down the stairs.

'I'm sorry, again,' Paloma told Mrs P. 'I'll be in touch tomorrow and we'll discuss further.'

'Come in,' Prendergast said, beckoning to my mother.

I mooched in behind her, pulling my fringe down over my face and curling my jumper over my hands.

'OK, so this is an indication of what we need to discuss today,' Prendergast began, passing my mother some pictures of me smoking, or rather, I was *holding* a cigarette, down by the back fence of the school.

'You're smoking now?' my mother said, looking puzzled. Mother knows I loathe smoking. I nag her every time she takes up the stupid hobby again.

'Hang on, that's not how it looks,' I said. 'I don't smoke. I was holding that cigarette for . . .'

I stopped mid-sentence. I was grassing up Striker. You don't do that to your friends. I've learned that from watching that show *The Bill.* If anything, you take the bullet for them.

'These, um, pictures have been photoshopped.' I mumbled lamely.

My mother just shook her head at me in disgust.

'Meanwhile, other news,' continued Mrs Prendergast. 'In Mathematics Poppet has leaped from a D grade to an A* virtually overnight!'

'Well that's fabulous, isn't it?' said Mother, perking up.

'No,' frowned Prendergast. 'Mr Douglas, Head of Maths, guesses that her work is being done by someone else. Whoever it was tried to imitate Poppet's writing but did such a bad job it looks like a small child's handwriting.'

'That's ridiculous . . .' began Mother, then her brain caught up with her. 'Oh, oh God. Flash.'

I stared intensely at my feet.

Prendergast seemed quite reasonable at this point, but the truth was she was simply gathering momentum.

'I'll be blunt with you, Mrs Montague-Jones,' she said, 'Poppet has given up on lessons. I took the liberty of conducting what we call at the Lycée an Emergency Pupil Investigation Survey and all the teachers said the same. Let me read you a few notes. Biology: Mr Abdul reports that Poppet does absolutely nothing in class aside from stare out of the window gossiping about boys with her friend, Blitzen Trapper.'

'What?!' I said. 'I can't STAND Blitzen Trapper. I never discuss boys with her!'

'Physical Education: Poppet is frequently absent from sports lessons. When she does attend them she frequently claims to be menstruating. Our records show she is currently menstruating at least twice a month and sometimes more. She is either lying or a modern medical miracle.'

'I say I've got my period so I don't have to go in the school shower,' I said, 'and get PERVED over by Mrs Dalrymple.'

'POPPET, BE QUIET,' my mother said.

'English,' Prendergast continued. 'Poppet's essays are bad to the point of surreal. She received a U grade recently for her *Wuthering Heights* essay that arrived three weeks late, covered in dog paw-prints and ketchup and trailed off midway through to discuss the TV show *Masterchef*.'

'But the book is very tense!' I said. 'I was describing other things that make me TENSE!'

No one was listening. Mrs Prendergast was standing by the window now. She'd picked up a pair of binoculars from the windowledge and clamped them to her face like a giant owl in a pinstriped suit, watching the playing fields where girls were moving between lessons.

'The point is, I am in the business of creating FUTURE LEADERS OF GREAT BRITAIN, Mrs Montague-Jones!' she said. 'And thirty-five years in education has taught me only too well that one bad apple turns the whole cart rotten. And can I remind you how much you've spent on Poppet's education since Year Seven, Mrs Montague-Jones?'

'Mmm?' said Mummy. I don't think she really did.

Prendergast shifted back to her laptop and tapped a few keys.

'With school fees, equipment, foreign excursions and other extra-curricular activities, the total to date is . . . one hundred and forty-seven thousand pounds.'

'Christ on a bike,' my mother said.

I looked sheepishly out of the window.

'OK . . . OK . . . perhaps Poppet isn't *academically* gifted,' said my mother. 'But her talent lies in art! Poppet's sculpture has been exhibited at the ICA.'

'Ah, Poppet's art,' tutted Prendergast, re-examining the file. 'Apparently Poppet's GCSE piece, a nude Greek god, has remained untouched since before Christmas.'

'Oh I'm sick to death of thinking about that thing,' I said. 'I started working on the willy last month and I chipped too hard on the base and it snapped off. It's ruined!'

'Well, make him without a willy!' Mother said.

'What?' I said, 'Just have him standing there with a big hole instead of a willy?'

'Well how important is the willy?' my mother said, looking to Prendergast for advice. 'Is the willy crucial?'

'I don't know anything about the sculpture's *appendage*,'

stuttered Prendergast. 'I'm talking about Poppet's disregard for her Art GCSE generally, which seemed to coincide with the arrival of her new BOYFRIEND.'

Well this was the point when the meeting really began to unravel. The blood in my veins temporarily froze.

'Poppet doesn't have a boyfriend,' Mother said. 'I would know if she did.'

'Peculiar,' Prendergast replied, 'because my intelligence tells me she's been dating a young man for over three months. Didn't you know?'

'No I did not,' Mother said, swivelling round and staring at me. 'You've got a boyfriend? Does she mean Felix Hayes-Burlington from across the road?'

'No, it's not him,' Prendergast said. 'I know Felix's father, Dr Hayes-Burlington, they're a lovely family. No, I'm talking about *this* boy.'

Then Prendergast played her killer card. She opened my file and pushed another photo across the desk. A photo of me snogging Kwame Kobina at the end of a road about half a mile away from the school. My cheeks were going burgundy.

I realized it had been taken about two weeks ago, on the day I skived off from my after-school sculpting lesson and we took the bus to Vue in Kilburn to see *Dead Days* with Robert Pattinson. You could actually see my tongue in Kwame's mouth and his hand on my bum.

My mother's lips went very hard and small like she'd just eaten a rabbit poo mistaking it for liquorice.

'Oh, Poppet,' she groaned. 'NO . . . no, no, no, no, no! It's that hooligan from the Cottingham Estate isn't it? That bloody boy? Isn't it? ISN'T IT? What did I tell you? YOU'VE BEEN HANGING AROUND THAT DAMNED COTTINGHAM ESTATE WITH DRUG DEALERS AND GANGSTERS AGAIN!'

'Ah, this boy is from the Cottingham Estate in Kilburn?' Prendergast said, as if the final clue in the puzzle of my terrible behaviour had been slotted into place. 'Well this makes sense. We've also got evidence of the very same boy picking up Striker Earhart by car after school, which directly contravenes school rules. Striker has just been exluded for six weeks.'

'What are you talking about now? Kwame doesn't have a car,' I said. 'You're all mental. MENTAL.'

Prendergast passed more photos across the table; this time of Striker in the front seat of a black Golf GTI beside a black guy with short hair wearing a furry coat. It wasn't Kwame, it was Bizzle from the New Year's Eve party. *Striker has been seeing Bizzle.*

'That's not the same person,' I snapped. 'They're just both black. There's more than one black boy in London.'

'Oh, who is this boy then?' said Prendergast.

'I don't know,' I lied.

I don't recall the finer details of the meeting after that. I was too consumed with rage. I remember calling both Mummy and Prendergast racists and accusing them of making me live under a fascist dictatorship. (Knute says that a lot, it always sounds enormously warlike and impressive.) I know I definitely grabbed the photo of Kwame and I snogging, and yelled something about Prendergast having no right to own pictures of me without my consent. Then I ripped one of the sheets of paper covered in photos into little pieces and chucked it about like confetti, then sat there sulking with paper all over my head like a total berk.

I've been excluded from Lycée for three weeks. Within that time I have got to catch up with work and change my attitude or I'm out, permanently.

The car journey home was eerily silent. Mummy didn't say a word.

She hasn't said anything to me all evening, either, although I heard her bickering with Daddy on iCam and the word 'Cottingham' came up many times.

My parents can't decide how to punish me. This makes things feel much worse.

I am, in their eyes, beyond control.

FEBRUARY

FEBRUARY

POPPET ZANZIBAR MONTAGUE-JONES'S BEHAVIOURAL CONTRACT

Due to incessant lying and general dishonest behaviour, we, your parents Jocasta and James Montague-Jones have no choice other than to issue you with this behavioural contract. You are at liberty to reject the specified terms and conditions, however we must remind you that failure to sign this agreement and live within its restrictions will result in immediate and complete disinheritance from all Montague-Jones wealth. Terms of this contract are non-negotiable and will remain in operation until further notice.

Please read the following clauses carefully and, if you are in agreement, add a date and signature in the space below:

- *Poppet Zanzibar Montague-Jones is to be grounded indefinitely. All excursions outside of 1 Octavia Square must be pre-agreed by Jocasta Montague-Jones or a specified guardian i.e. Kitten Calypso Montague-Jones.*

- *Striker Earhart, Vixen Blaise Diaz-Brocklehurst and any*

other friends are prohibited from visiting the house or travelling in the same car as Poppet.

- *Poppet is to be driven to all appointments and returned home by the named driver, Voychek Dribozki. On absolutely no account must Poppet travel by herself on public transport or attempt to travel anywhere on foot.*

- *Poppet's usage of iPhone, internet and landline telephone will be at the sole discretion of Jocasta Montague-Jones until further notice.*

- *Poppet's credit card and debit cards are to be confiscated. Expenditure for absolute necessities will be allocated at the discretion of Jocasta Montague-Jones. All receipts must be supplied for inspection.*

- *Usage of alcohol, cigarettes and all drugs are completely prohibited.*

- *Bad language will NOT be tolerated in any form.*

- *Poppet will concentrate wholly on her studies and endeavour to lift all of her grades to a C or above in time for the GCSE exams. She will improve her attitude to her studies and private tuition and show willingness to LEARN.*

- *Poppet will understand that this contract is as inconvenient and painful for her parents as it is for herself, but it was her own UNRULY AND FERAL actions that have caused this situation.*

Signed .... *Signed* ....

TUESDAY 2ND FEBRUARY

3 A.M. 1 OCTAVIA SQUARE

GGNGNGNGNGNGNG OH MY GOD I HATE THEM. I hate them hate them hate them. There's no point in being alive. NONE. Not if I have to live here with these hideous vile unreasonable monsters. That's it. I'm getting in touch with a lawyer FIRST THING in the morning to begin divorce proceedings against the whole ruddy Montague-Jones family. Yes – that's right – I'm DIVORCING the whole hellish lot of them and telling my lawyer to give a statement saying, 'Oh, and by the way, Poppet is now Poppet Plimpton and she has REJECTED the family name and she NEVER EVER EVER EVER wants to see any of you again, no matter how much you all weep and boo-hoo and plead. GO AWAY!' And Mummy will say, 'Oh, does she mean me?!' and the lawyer will say, 'Yes, Jocasta, Poppet especially means you as you're a total EVIL COW!' NO, hang on, what I'm going to do is divorce my family and then kill myself. YES THAT'S IT, KILL MYSELF by chucking myself off a very

very big high bridge somewhere desolate and remote, and I'll drown in a river and my body will eventually wash up on a beach in France all bloated and bruised from being bashed about in the sea for five weeks, and one of them will have to identify my corpse and it will be ENORMOUSLY TRAUMATIC. And at the funeral my family will be going, 'OH LORKS O' LORDY – we wish we'd never been so horrid to poor Poppet now. We fully understand now that she was in the right and we were being MASSIVE TURDS treating her that way . . .' EXCEPT THEY WON'T BE ABLE TO COME TO THE FUNERAL as I shall leave a handwritten letter BANNING THEM ALL FROM COMING TO IT. Yes, I'll tell them all to stay away AND UP IN HEAVEN I'LL LAUGH MY SOCKS OFF AT THEM CRYING. And then I'll haunt them from beyond the grave so every time they walk into rooms in this stupid bloody house light bulbs will explode or vases will fall off mantlepieces. Yes, I'LL BE A GHOST PUNISHING THEM ALL, eternally. Because I hate them all, HATE THEM. I wish they were all dead. I wish I was dead. How can they force me to sign a contract?? What kinds of freaks make their child sign a contract?? TOTAL FREAKS, THAT'S WHO. This is SOOOO LIKE COMPLETELY TOTALLY CHILD ABUSE. I'M RINGING SOCIAL WORKERS IN THE MORNING AND TELLING THEM EVERY SINGLE DETAIL. I hope they lock my mother up. OH RUDDY NORA? I CAN'T EVEN USE THE PHONE to call the police, can I? It was in that stupid contract. Holy mother of Satan, those two idiots who call themselves my parents have literally RUINED MY LIFE. Well I think they're totally sad. They shouldn't have had me if they HATE CHILDREN SO MUCH. They shouldn't have had me if they have such obvious mental-health issues. THEY ONLY HAD ME AS THEY HATE THEMSELVES AND NEED SOMEONE ELSE TO HATE. This is a one hundred per cent true fact. Well, I'm running away from home first thing in the morning (after breakfast, as Mrs Minsk is making kedgeree and that's my favourite) and I swear I'm going to live under a bridge for a while and smoke lots of crack and get pregnant by a tramp before I divorce the whole ruddy Montague-Jones clan and then leap off the top of Big Ben and land in the Thames and I HOPE THEY'RE HAPPY, THE BLOODY RUDDY BIG PIGS.

5 A.M.

Maybe I should calm down. My throat hurts from crying.

FRIDAY 5TH FEBRUARY

So far I've been grounded for four days but it feels like ten long years. This is all so totally unfair. I spent an hour this morning crying about this in the kitchen while Mrs Minsk loaded the dishwasher and made a birdcake to feed the robins and sparrows in the garden. Mrs Minsk doesn't believe in buying bird feed from the pet shop. She makes her own from cereal and lard and bits of bacon rind and then pours it into a tupperware box to set. It's the most vile thing ever but the birds love it. Kitten and I used to dare each other to eat bits of it when we were little.

Mrs Minsk is the only person willing to listen to me right now when I'm complaining about the hideousness of my life. I think she's the only person vaguely sympathetic to the fact that it was ruddy Striker Earhart who was caught shoplifting on CCTV at Bodwin's Boutique, not me. But now I'm the one being treated like the ruddy criminal. And it was Striker Earhart lying to her mother saying she was staying at my house with me and then sneaking off with Bizzle and going off to all-night parties. I didn't even know about it. Striker was lying to me too! But now the crap has hit the fan, I'm being being punished like I'm guilty of all those things too. I now know the true meaning of the phrase 'tarred with the same brush'.

And the very worst thing is, that because I'm forbidden to speak to Striker, we can't even get our ruddy stories straight to lie. Mother keeps appearing in my peripheral vision with a huge red face and eyes like pieces of coal, fresh from another long phone call with Paloma Earhart, hurling another string of accusations at me. And the more I stumble over my answers and contradict Striker's lies the worse this whole mess becomes.

'And I can't believe you'd even drag Felix's mother into your web of deceit!' Mother shouted at me this morning. 'You've sunk to the lowest level now, young lady! I spoke to Persephone Hayes-Burlington and she says you weren't with Felix on the two times you apparently went to the cinema with him. Felix was with another girl. His new girlfriend Coco!'

I glowered back at my mother. I tried to speak, but couldn't. Then I went upstairs and curled in a ball under my duvet. In a nutshell, I wanted the world to stop as I was sick to the stomach with it. Who the hell is Coco? Who is this girl? There are no Cocos in our circle of friends. Oh why should I care? Actually I don't care. This is me not caring. Suck it up.

I've got to give my mother credit for one thing though, of all the ruddy stupid rules in that behavioural contract designed to annoy me, making Voychek my permanent chauffeur was a work of evil genius. Mother knows I bloody hate Voychek. I had several arguments with this stupid ruddy man last year when he was sticking his beak into my private business and reporting back to Mummy all the things he noticed when driving me.

'Poppet, you told me it was GIRLS ONLY at Tabitha's sleepover?' Mother would say. 'So why does Voychek claim he saw two boys sitting on her garden wall at eleven p.m., and one of them was carrying a set of climbing crampons as if he was going to scale the side of the house?' Well Tabitha got totally busted for that and Luca and Titus from Godspeed Boys' Academy were excluded for a week for 'darkening the school name'.

And if I ever say I'm going to the cinema and need to be picked up, Voychek is the only driver who would call Vue switchboard and double-check what time the movie actually finishes so we can't hang about in the foyer and flirt with boys in the Haagen-Dazs café and have any real fun.

Once upon a time Voychek used to be in the Polish military and he clearly still ruddy thinks he is and that his whole life is one big secret spying mission and I'm the BLOODY ENEMY HE'S TRYING TO DEFEAT.

And now I've got to see him every day. Or stare at the back of his exceptionally wide brainless head and behold his terrifyingly hairy ears as he drives about Hampstead listening to Talk London FM radio, agreeing frantically with all the mental things grown-ups call in to talk to the DJ about. For example, someone will call in and say, 'We should send all the immigrants back to the country they came from in a boat. They ruin our country.'

And Voychek will nod furiously and say, 'Yes, yes, this iz good idea, a big boat. Send them all back!'

So then I tut loudly and say, 'Voychek, you're from Poland, YOU'RE AN IMMIGRANT, that means they would send you back too!'

Voychek tuts and says, 'No, not me, I pay good tax and build your hospital and schools. They mean scrounger from Africa.'

So I just sit in silence, fuming, thinking about Kwame's mother who has worked two jobs and sometimes three jobs at a time since she came to Britain and always pays her tax. But I say nothing, as I'm beginning to realize my mouth gets me into a lot of trouble.

And the irritating thing is, at least if Voychek is driving me about then I'm still permitted the odd 'treat' like attending my ICA sculpting course or getting out of the car unaccompanied at the organic grocers in Hampstead and picking up Puy lentils and wild rice for Kitten. These type of things are the highlight of my life right now.

And, oh God, I miss Kwame so much. He doesn't even know properly what has happened to me. I only managed to get one short text message out to him before my phone was taken that said: TOTALLY GROUNDED, WILL CALL YOU. But then the phone was put in the family vault and they've changed the bloody passcode so I can't even bribe Flash to get it for me.

I've been lying in bed for hours on end wearing Kwame's beanie hat. It's the one that I borrowed when it was snowing before Christmas and we went to Hampstead Heath and had a snowball fight. It smells of the sweet coconuty hair fudge that he uses. I've been lying under the duvet with the hat pulled down, sniffing the wool. It makes my heart go all wonky. What the hell can I do?

Mummy came into my room last night and sat down on the side of my bed. It was just after we'd had another screaming row about the Cottingham Estate and why I can never see Kwame ever again. She grabbed my hand and said, 'Do you ever think for one single minute how much this is killing me too, Poppet? Do you realize that?'

'Whatever,' I said, scrunching my hand up really hard so she couldn't play with my fingers or think I like her at all because I don't, I loathe her.

'I'm having a terrible time too, Poppet,' she said. 'I don't like seeing you so wretched and miserable. But I have to do something. I turned a blind eye to Kitten's behaviour and it's still smacking me in the face every time I open a newspaper. It doesn't matter that Kitten is doing so well now, all anybody wants to read is that she was once a drug addict and that I'm a terrible failure as a mother. Kitten has to deal with that stigma every day too!'

'Hmmm,' I grumped.

'Kitten could have died or ended up in prison the way she was headed,' Mother said. 'Do you blame me for trying to save you from that?'

'I don't need saving,' I said, stomping over to the window ledge and placing my head against the cold glass, then banging it a few times as the distraction of the pain felt almost soothing.

'Well I just want you to know that I'm not happy either,' my mother said.

'Whatever.' I scowled at her. 'Can you please leave now and shut the door?'

Mother did this without another word. At first this felt

like I'd won, but after around another ten minutes sitting there with no phone and the wi-fi turned off so I can't iChat or email anyone I remembered again that it's me who's the absolute loser in all this.

I told Mrs Minsk all of that this morning and she thought for a while and said, 'Your mother no trust you at the moment. You need to rebuild trust. It's not impossible, just hard work.'

I told Mrs Minsk I have no energy left for hard work right now. I simply want to die and be thrown in a hole.

'So this Kwame boy is good boy then?' Mrs Minsk said, as we were walking out into the garden feeding the spare breadcrumbs and nuts to the squirrels who are living in the oak trees.

'Yes! He's a very good boy!' I told her. 'That's the annoying thing. He's a straight A student. He's going to be a doctor.'

'Then why you keep him secret? It makes him look like a bad boy. Like that Buzzybee boy? Striker's boyfriend.'

'Bizzle,' I corrected her, although the name Buzzybee was making me smile a bit for the first time in five days.

'So why you never invite Kwame here?' she asked.

'I did! But it all went wrong,' I said.

'Why, what did he do wrong?' Mrs Minsk said.

'No, it wasn't him, it was all of them,' I said pointing at the house. 'He came to the Christmas drinks party, but he only stayed like ten minutes. It was a disaster. They were all being freaks, as usual.'

'Well maybe he needs to come again and everyone be on best behaviour,' said Mrs Minsk.

I just sighed when she said that. The fact is there's no way Mummy will let Kwame in the house again. He's from the Cottingham Estate. He might steal her best candle holders and run off down Kilburn High Street with them in his underpants and swap them for a kilo of mephedrone, mightn't he? That's what people like Kwame do, ISN'T IT?

THURSDAY 11TH FEBRUARY

The most extraordinary thing occurred today. I'm not entirely certain how I feel about it. I can't work out if I'm massively lucky or if Mummy is being very, very devious indeed. And I can't say a word to her about it as then she'll know that I've sussed she's being devious and I will NOT give her the pleasure. Safe to say, however, I'm utterly freaked out.

The day started out boringly enough with a morning of chi yoga and trigonometry, followed by a whole afternoon being held hostage by Kitten in the dining room ploughing through the novel *Wuthering* ruddy *Heights,* watching DVD clips of the BBC version of *Wuthering Heights,* then listening to an MP3 playing a song called *Wuthering Heights* by a woman called Kate Bush, which was a lot of hideous screeching. She sounded like she had a tampon in at a difficult angle.

Finally, after all this deep joy, I was allowed outdoors for a trip to my dentist, Mr Banderas, to have my top brace tightened as it keeps wobbling when I speak and getting raspberry jam pips caught in it, which go rotten and smell.

I can't think of a worse way to spend an afternoon. This was worse than that time Vixen and I went to the matinée performance of the musical *Cats*, which was song after song about kippers and mice sang by people in stick-on whiskers, coughing up hairballs.

By the time I was in the dentist's chair this afternoon and Mr Banderas was headed towards me with that big, metal twisty-turny torture device he liked to attack me with I was in the grip of a rather volatile form of depression.

'You may find this a touch uncomfortable,' Banderas said, before grabbing my lips and dragging them apart, inserting his entire upper body inside my head then poking about with all the finesse of an angry water buffalo.

'Mghghghgh, I'm completely sick of wearing this thing,' I moaned as he finally came up for air. 'How much longer now?'

'Six months,' Banderas said. 'It'll pass by in no time.'

'Pgh,' I said. 'Can't we just take them out now? Today? I hate them. I don't care what my teeth look like. And they hurrrrrrt.'

'No,' he said, 'and besides, your mother called the nurse this morning and said under no account to remove them whatever you tell us. She says they don't hurt and you never mention them.'

'But they do hurrrrrrt,' I whined. Even I knew I was whining. I could hear my voice making a squeaky, sing-song sound. I was irritating myself.

'Where do they hurt?' he said, patiently.

'All over,' I said. 'And they make me look hideous!'

'You can barely see anything,' he said.

'Barely see anything?' I said, chomping my metal teeth at him. 'Look at me? I look like something Doctor Who chases and zaps with a sonic screwdriver!'

'No you don't,' he said, 'and any inconvenience now will be worth it longterm. Poppet, I have clients coming in here aged thirty-eight, demanding I set their teeth straight. By then it's a huge job. You don't want to be one of those people.'

I sighed loudly when he said that. 'Why should I care what I'll think when I'm thirty-eight?' I said. 'I'll be dead by then anyway. My aim is to live fast, die middle-aged and leave a hot Cougar corpse.'

Mr Banderas laughed for about five minutes when I said that. I think being grounded and excluded from school has sent me a bit insane. The most curious things keep popping out of my mouth, like my brain feels it has absolutely nothing to lose.

'You're very funny, Poppet,' he said. 'But I won't be

removing the braces. Your mother hasn't consented and she's the one who has paid over twelve grand in orthodontal fees so far. She who pays the piper calls the tune, as they say.'

'Holy hell, it's my mouth,' I grumbled. 'This is like living under a fascist dictatorship!'

'Well, not really,' Bandares said. 'Y'know I grew up in Chile under the dictatorship of General Pinochet. He was quite keen on killing and torture and human rights abuses. This isn't really like that at all.'

'Oh you know what I mean, Mr Banderas,' I said, rolling my eyes.

'Yes, I know what you mean, kiddo.' He ruffled my hair like he used to when I was six.

'I'm just tired of people treating me like a little girl,' I complained. Mr B. wasn't really listening to me now.

'OK, my four p.m. appointment is here now. Would you like a lollipop for being such a good patient?' he said.

'Yes please,' I said. 'I'll have a strawberry one.'

As I walked out of the dentist's, sucking my lollipop, Voychek was waiting for me in the temporary parking bay, standing by the bonnet of his Mercedes. He opened the back door of the Merc and chivvied me in saying, 'We need to get home as soon as possible. Your mother says you have guest.'

'A guest?' I said. 'I'm not allowed guests. Who?'

'I don't know this information,' he said, which

sounded unfeasible as Voychek knows more about the inner-runnings of 1 Octavia Square than the family does. I ignored this news as I thought it was probably a prank on my mother's part, fooling me into actually looking forward to anything.

I sat in silence all the way home listening to a phone-in on Talk London about whether Britain should ban Islamic women wearing burkhas in public. Voychek thought yes, as he thinks burkhas are scary. I laughed when he said that. The fact that Voychek, who looks like he has bodies buried under his patio, is 'scared' of a woman in a floor-length sheet is mindboggling. But we agree to differ on some matters like this as journeys go a lot smoother when we're both faking being vaguely chums.

However, as we turned the corner into Octavia Square the mood in the car degenerated rapidly.

'Who is that? At front door? Who?' said Voychek, pulling a rather abrupt emergency stop in the road.

'What?' I said, thanking God I was wearing a seatbelt or I'd have ended up splattered all over the front windscreen.

'That boy,' he said. 'Boy on front step. Black boy!'

'What boy?' I said. 'Oh . . . my . . . God.'

Standing on the front doorstep of 1 Octavia Square, ringing the doorbell and checking his watch, was Kwame Kobina. *My Kwame*, stood there bold as brass. He didn't look like he was sneaking a chance to see me or do anything underhand. He looked completely sure of himself, like he had an appointment. As I looked closer I noticed he was wearing a crisp, white shirt, a grey tie and smart black trousers, like he was going for an interview with the board of an investment bank in the City.

By this point Voychek was bashing keys on his phone furiously trying to get hold of my mother.

'I tell your mother not to open the door,' he said. 'It confidence trickster! She needs to put up the security gates.'

'Oh chill out, Voychek,' I snapped. 'I know this boy, let me out of the car.'

'No,' said Voychek, like I was an imbecile. 'No! It's dangerous.'

'Let me out, Voychek!' I shouted, 'It's Kwame. He's my bloody boyfriend. Let me out to see him. Voychek, open the bloody doors!'

'I'm not letting you out,' he said, 'I no like look of this person.'

Well my rage level flipped over into CODE RED then. A entire week of anger came flooding up to the surface, my face was hot and scarlet.

'LET ME OUT OF THIS CAR!' I shouted, kicking the back of his seat. 'Turn off the ruddy childlocks now or I'll kick this ruddy window out with my foot.'

OK, I can't believe I said this either. It was at this very moment I suddenly understood fully why Kitten used to do and say so many terrible things during her bad years. Because the more badly behaved you are, the more they treat you like a child, and the more they treat you like a child, the more enormously badly behaved you are through sheer frustration. In the end you just go loopy, ga-ga, insane.

'Go ahead, kick it, it triple-strength bullet-proof glass,' Voychek said. 'You just break your foot. Try if you want.'

Well at that point, thankfully, the front door opened and my mother appeared. I watched with my mouth hanging wide open as Mummy shook hands politely with Kwame as if he was a client, then they exchanged small talk about the ornamental spiral trees in large bronze pots we have by the front door. Then Mother noticed the Merc and waved, shouting, 'Hi, Poppet! Kwame is here.'

I began to suspect I'd actually gone so insane I was hallucinating. Or I'd fallen asleep at the dentist's and this was all an eerily vivid dream. Kwame was on my doorstep dressed like a thirty-year-old, and my mother was smiling at him, and Voychek was unlocking the childlocks and opening the door and chivvying me out of the car to meet them. I placed my feet unsteadily on the ground and walked towards the house, feeling enormously giddy and vomitous.

'Hello, Kwame,' I said.

'Hello, Poppet.'

Kwame's eyes were trying to say a mixture of, 'I'm sorry' and, 'I know this is weird' and, 'I am so pleased to see you' all at once. Mine were saying 'What is going on? I am freaking out big time!'

'Kwame was just saying he's working towards a place at Queen Mary's now for his medical training,' Mummy said, as I followed them both into the hallway, shaking my head in disbelief. 'Isn't that super? I'm almost certain Granny is firm chums with President of the London School of Medicine so we must put in a word and ensure you get a place, y'know, even if you have a rough exam day.'

'Mpghhghgh,' I said.

Kwame's eyes lit up. 'Oh my dayz,' he said, like this was the first time he thought this kind of thing was possible. Of course it is. All rich people do it. I felt ashamed already and he'd only been inside the house forty seconds.

'Let's convene in the lounge,' Mummy said, like this was the most natural thing in the world. I'm sure she was enjoying messing with my head.

'Can I ask Mrs Minsk to bring us some coffee?' said Mummy.

'Coffee would be wonderful, thank you, Mrs Montague-Jones,' Kwame replied, using this weird voice I've never heard him do before. It didn't have any of the Cockney or slight African lilt that I love.

'Why are you wearing a tie, Kwame?' I whispered loudly. 'What are you doing here? What is going on?'

Kwame scrunched his brow as if to say: *Shhh, don't ruin this. Be quiet.*

'What are you doing here?' I said, louder this time.

'So anyway, Kwame,' Mummy said, ignoring my fuss. 'As I was saying on the phone, and I hope you don't mind me calling you out of the blue, but your name was on Poppet's phone, which has been in my handbag for a week, so I took the liberty of calling it.'

'No, it's fine,' he said.

'Well I mind!' I said. 'Can I have the phone back now? Who else have you been calling?'

'Now,' said Mummy, blanking out my noise. 'I've been thinking deeply about the situation with Poppet's schooling. As you know, Poppet is lagging terribly far behind in lessons. Her GCSE courses are in total chaos.'

'Yes, I know.' Kwame nodded.

I was consumed with shame now. I've hidden all of this from Kwame. I never ever wanted him to know just how stupid I really was. This was terrible.

'And at the moment,' continued Mummy. 'Poppet has several pieces of coursework classed as unsubmitted, and in English and Maths she's fallen so far behind that Hampstead Lycée aren't even sure whether to enter her for the GCSEs.'

Kwame and Mummy both looked at each other with expressions that seemed to say, *Whatever will we do with her?*

'I'm here you know,' I said, banging one of the sofa cushions with my hand. 'Talk *to* me, not *about* me.'

'Stop being deliberately obtuse Poppet.' Mummy

frowned. 'We're trying to help you.'

'What do you mean, "We"?' I said, 'What's going on?'

'Well you keep insisting you want to spend time with Kwame,' said Mother. 'And you've told me a million times he's a straight A student and completely trustworthy!'

'I do!' I said. 'He is!'

'Well OK,' she said. 'I didn't listen to you at first as I was rather outraged by all the lying.' Mummy turned to Kwame now, saying, 'You can understand that can't you, Kwame? Poppet has been lying an enormous amount.'

'I told her not to lie Mrs Montague-Jones,' said Kwame in his weird not-Kwame voice.

'Oh shut up, Kwame,' I said, starting to lose patience with him, sitting there in his stupid tie, looking like someone who'd be on the telly talking about mortgages.

'I'm sure you weren't involved in the lying, Kwame, you seem like a very decent boy,' said my mother. 'And that's why I thought it would be a good idea to ask you to help with Poppet's tutoring.'

There was a terrible silence. Kwame looked at me, then stared directly at the floor.

Mummy smiled at me, waiting for my response.

'You're kidding me?' I said.

'No,' said Mummy. 'Kwame said he'd be delighted to help out. We've been thinking about three nights after school each week. Kwame feels confident he can get your grades up past C level. And I'll be around to support you too! I've postponed that contract in Seville as I want to be near you during this difficult time.'

I stared hard at Kwame. He was examining his fingernails now, which is what he does when he's nervous.

'And just to double-check, one hundred and fifty pounds a week is fine, Kwame?' said Mother. 'We can renegotiate if not? I know how expensive all those medical textbooks are going to be when you reach university.'

Kwame winced when she said that.

'One hundred and fifty pounds is great, thank you, Mrs Montague-Jones,' he said, then resumed examining his cuticles.

'Marvellous,' said Mother. 'Oh I am pleased!'

Very soon after that, before Kwame and I had any chance to chat privately, my mother turfed him out ever-so politely saying, 'Well we shan't keep you, I'm sure you've got lots of homework you need to do! See you next Monday, Kwame! Enchaaaaanted to meet you!' before closing the door and saying, 'Oh Poppet, what a darling boy? Isn't he an absolute joy! And from the Cottingham Estate too. Who knew people like that even existed there!'

I sat in the lounge for a long time after he'd gone, deadly still like a stone carving, trying to come to terms with what had just occurred.

My mother approves of Kwame and is paying him to

spend time with me and teach me quadratic equations. That's weird, isn't it? I'm not just imagining it? That's really weird. ISN'T IT?

'But I thought this would make you happy, Poppet!' Mummy smiled as she was leaving for her Royal Ballet gala dinner tonight. 'Good golly, young lady, there's no pleasing you is there?!'

I stared at her and said nothing. I wouldn't give her the pleasure of a reaction. I am completely weirded out by this and I can't even say why precisely. I'm allowed to see my beloved, gorgeous, kind Kwame three times a week. And from tomorrow I'm even allowed my iPhone back to make 'limited phonecalls for the forseeable future'. So although my credit cards are still missing and Voychek is still stalking me on every trip outdoors, I'm definitely in a three hundred per cent rosier position than I was. So why do I have this feeling I've been slightly stitched up?

FRIDAY 12TH FEBRUARY

Following a lot of inner contemplation I've decided to chill out about the Kwame thing. It felt so ruddy extraordinarily amazing yesterday to see him and smell him and be within grabbing distance of him that I shouldn't complain if the situation is a bit, well, freaky.

And at least it means Kwame still loves me and hasn't forgotten me if he wants to come three times a week and help me pass my GCSEs. Musn't it? That part's not freaky. Is it? And it's not THAT freaky that he's being paid by Mummy, is it? Oh God, no that's still totally FREAKY. That's ALWAYS freaky.

Actually, the best thing to do is not think so much about it and concentrate on nice things like the glorious remergence into public life of my iPhone. Yes, Hosannah on High! Let joy be unconfined! It is back! When I opened my eyes at nine a.m. this morning it was the first thing I saw, sitting like an old, loyal friend on the bedside table. Kitten or Mummy must have snuck in and put it back as I was snoring.

'Oh darling I've missed you so,' I said, clasping its slim black body to my chest, then clamping its cold, kissable screen to my face. 'We shall never be parted ever, ever again,' I cried, smothering it in love.

The phone was fully charged but missing a ton of text messages and emails, which I'm guessing my mother read and then deleted in a fit of pique last week.

I jumped out of bed and paced around the room holding it, feeling fifty times more alive and relevant as part of the human race than I did while it was confiscated.

Who to call first? Who? Kwame? No. I wasn't sure what to say to him right now. Striker Earhart? Yes! I needed to speak to Striker right then before someone grown up decided she was on a banned list.

I hit speed dial four and clamped the phone to my

face, my heart thumping in my chest. On connection, Striker's phone rang out about five times with a long high tone, which told me she wasn't in Great Britain, then I heard a clunk, like she'd picked up and dropped the phone into a sink or something, then a long ecstatic scream, and then four words which were quite rude and unrepeatable and then lots more laughing.

'Poppet Zanzibar Montague-Jones! My darling girl!' she screamed. 'You've got your phone back!? Hahaha FIGHT THE POWER! Hey, guess where I am? Guess? Go on guess?'

'I don't know! Somewhere far away. Not in Britain?' I said.

'Yes!'

'Where are you?' I said.

'SWITZERLAND,' she hooted. 'I'm so badly behaved Mother has actually had me deported.'

'Switzerland? Why Switzerland? That is so massively random,' I gasped. 'When did you go to Switzerland?'

'Nine, ruddy long days ago,' Striker said. 'Poppet, this is an emergency. I am being held captive in a chalet halfway up a bloody Swiss Alp by my loopy Godmother, Orphelia. Y'know the woman with the chin hair who my mother studied Psychotherapy with in California? I'm with her. She specialized in problem children so she offered to take me for a month to "rehabilitate me". I'm in rehab in Switzerland! It sounds sort of glamorous, doesn't it? But OH MY GOD I am dying of boredom.

Literally. There's nothing but snow for a million miles. And Orphelia doesn't even have a television. There's just a library of books. She says I should sit by the fire and read some classic fiction and "come to terms with recent events and open my mind to change".'

'Holy hell,' I said.

'And I'm forced, seriously FORCED, to have a two-hour Skype conversation with my mother every evening while she psycho-analyses me and makes me talk about my "problems". Poppet, I haven't got any ruddy problems aside from the ones *she*'s causing me. And . . . AND . . . my parents have joined forces and cancelled all of my credit cards. I have no money, at all. NONE. I am poor. Like a normal-girl-in-a-normal-world style POOR.'

'Me too,' I said. 'And they're threatening to disinherit me if I don't start behaving. Mummy says she'll instruct the lawyers to distribute most of my millions between Kitten, Knute, Flash and Dragon and use the rest to build a school in Liberia. In the meantime, I don't even have a penny.'

'This is disgusting! They're making us live like muggles,' shouted Striker. 'I loathe them all.'

It was so good to hear Striker's voice and hear her being bolshy again.

'Hey listen, Popz,' she said. 'Two nights ago I escaped and tried to get down the mountain and find the main road. I ran across a field, found a track and started running down it but it was snowing like crazy! Big massive flakes falling sideways and I couldn't see and and I was wearing a skirt and a batwing jumper and I kept falling over and my mimsy was frozen and my knickers were full of icicles. It was ridiculous.'

'Striker, you can't escape from anywhere in Switzerland in just a skirt,' I laughed. 'It's not *The Sound of Music.* You need hiking gear. Like an explorer.'

'I know that *now,* Poppet,' she said. 'But I had to take my chance though. Seriously, I'm about to kill someone. Oh my God, here's an idea, Popz!' said Striker, her voice brightening. 'Get on a flight and come to Switzerland. Oh go on. Do it, please. Fly to Berne and meanwhile I'll make a snowboard out of old cereal packets and slide down the Alps and hitch to meet you. We'll check into a suite at the Bellevue Palace and ring room service and order gallons of champagne and have heaps of fun. We're already in tons of trouble. We may as well give them all something to really moan about.'

'We haven't any money, Striker,' I said.

'Oh . . . yes,' she said. 'OK, right, steal a credit card from your mother's purse. You might need to drug her first, but that's easy, just find those Valium pills she always has in the house and trick her into taking them. In our house, we mash pills up in tinned tuna when we want to fool the cat into eating them. Does your mother like tuna?'

'She likes sushi,' I said. 'Hang on. I'm NOT

DRUGGING MY MOTHER.'

'Sushi? That would work,' said Striker, ignoring me. 'Push the Valium into the salmon skin rolls, wait till her head is lolling about and her mouth open, drooling, swipe her black Amex, or whichever has the biggest limit on it, then book a flight out of Gatwick.'

'No,' I said. 'No no no. Thrice NO.'

'You're going to need a wig, and a change of clothing and . . . a fake passport as your normal one will alert the police if border control are looking for you. Actually, I know someone who hangs about with Bizzle who can get you a fake passport.'

'Striker.' I sighed, lying down again in bed and pulling the duvet up. 'I'm staying here.'

'Oh, Poppet, where's your spirit of adventure gone to?' she shouted.

'I never had a spirit of adventure!' I moaned. 'Well I had a tiny smattering of one but that's been destroyed underfoot by the military junta ruling this house.'

'Pah,' tutted Striker. 'They've broken you. This is what they want. Why are you letting them break you?'

'Striker,' I said, 'how can I *not* be broken? I've been indoors being shouted at for twelve days.'

'Oh, just ignore them,' she said. 'Half the stuff I'm in trouble for I didn't even do. It's competely made up. I'm just ignoring whatever they say. I should sue them for libel.'

I laughed loudly at this part. Striker honestly believed

she was being framed for crimes she didn't commit.

'Oh, thanks for saying you were staying here then staying out all night with Bizzle, by the way,' I said. 'You could have told me that was your story.'

'Hmmm. Yeah, sorry about about that,' she said. 'Bizzle wanted to take me to see Giggs perform at Pascha. I knew you'd tell me not to do it so I didn't mention it! Besides, it was the perfect plan. I got away with it for three whole weeks. No one would ever have known if you'd not handed in that stupid *Wuthering Heights* essay. The one with Garfield in it.'

'Ha! What has my Garfield essay got to do with this?' I said, gasping at her audacity.

'Well this is what started this period of hideousness!' quacked Striker. 'You handed in that essay, which just so happened to be the worst essay ever written in one hundred years or history of Hampstead Lycée for Young Ladies, which resulted in Prendergast launching an Emergency Pupil Investigation on you, which resulted in a photograph of you smoking.'

'I was holding YOUR CIGARETTE while you were on your iPhone,' I snapped back at her, thoroughly disgruntled.

'Oh let's not squabble over details,' said Striker. 'Whatever happened, Prendergast then started investigating us. That's how the Bizzle thing came to light. And now it's ruined. He's the most exciting boy I've ever met in my whole life and now it's ruined!

He's seeing someone else. The moment I left the country I was binned.'

I was feeling a bit guilty by now. Maybe this was my fault after all? I gave myself a shake.

'Oh you're good, Striker,' I laughed. 'You're very good. Look, you can twist and you can turn, but this is all your ruddy fault.'

Striker seemed distracted now.

'Ooh, oh my gosh, Poppet, a HUMAN BEING!' she said.

'Where?' I said.

'Someone just skiied down the hill outside the lodge. Another human being. I wonder if they have any fags? I'm gasping. Hey, bring me twenty Marlboro Lights!'

I was beginning to gather that Striker was treating her punishment in Switzerland as a huge joke.

'Right, must go,' said Striker. 'I can hear Orphelia's car. She actually believes my phone has no signal here and has let me keep it. Look, I'll be home within a week. There's no way Orphelia will stand me for much longer. I'm going to accidentally set fire to an armchair tonight when she lets me stoke the log fire. I'll be on a plane by Monday.'

'Striker, don't set fire to anything!' I said, but the phone had gone dead.

I lay in bed for a while thinking about Striker and about how her brain is wired so differently to mine, which makes her see life as one huge hilarious battle to be fought dirtily and rules only there to be broken. Then my phone started ringing again and the screen filled up with a picture of Vixen's pretty face. I pressed answer to hear the delicate sound of her sobbing.

'Poppet,' she said, 'I just ran into your mother in Fresh and Wild in Hampstead High Street. She told me she'd given you your phone back and I could call you. I just can't believe this has happened, it's a diabolical miscarriage of justice. It's just completely wrong.'

'Oh, don't worry, Vix. I'm fine. Just bored and rather cross. How are you? How is school? What am I missing?'

'School is hell without you both,' Vix said. 'Blitzen and Amelia are such loud, annoying beasts now that Striker isn't there to shut them up. And honestly, Poppet, you are like completely famous now. The last person to get excluded from Hampstead Lycée was Sontag Cranford two years ago when she went totally lezboid and started sending pervy letters to Miss Hazlett in Gym. Everyone is talking about it.'

'Saying what?' I said, starting to feel rather cold at the thought.

'Oh, most of it isn't even true.'

'Like what?' I said.

'Oh it's all nothing,' she stuttered. 'Just silly stuff. I shouldn't have said anything.'

'What silly stuff?' I persisted. 'Tell me.'

'Oh it's nothing anyone could take remotely seriously,' she said. 'Oh I feel like an idiot now. I've upset you even more. I am such a terrible idiot.'

'Vixen, tell me what the rumour is about me!' I said. 'I won't be upset at you.'

'Oh it's just that you're, well, um, pregnant,' she said.

I squeaked in horror, 'What?'

'Pregnant . . . again,' she continued. 'As in, this is your second child.'

'What? How? Who's saying this?' I said. 'Who was my first child? I haven't had any children. I've never even ruddy done it with anyone!'

'That's what I've been telling people,' Vixen said, emphatically, 'I've been telling people you've never even done it with anyone!'

'Oh God,' I groaned. The thought that every pupil at Hampstead Lycée for Young Ladies was in deep discussion over whether Poppet Montague-Jones has or hasn't ever done it with a boy yet was making my toes curl so much they'd retracted into my feet and created centurion-style hooves.

'How can I have already had one baby? It makes no sense.'

'Well some girls are saying that Dragon is actually your son,' Vixen said. 'And that your mother made up that story about bringing him from Liberia. And that time last year when you were a bit heavier, well people are saying you actually had a baby growing under your school jumper.'

'I was just fat,' I said. 'I was eating a lot of Krispy

Kreme donuts and not doing any exercise!'

'That's what I said,' said Vixen. 'Well, I didn't say you were fat. You weren't fat. You were just, y'know, more generously covered than you are now. But in a nice way. You suit being bigger. I mean, voluptuous. Oh crikey, I wish I'd not told you this.'

Vixed sniffed a big sniff. She sounded more heartbroken about this than me, I was just irate.

'And I'm pregnant again now, am I?' I said. 'Well, haven't I been busy!?'

'Well, there's a silly rumour that in cross-country running last month, you were hanging right behind at the back as you could feel the baby kicking.'

'I'm always at the back during running,' I said. 'There are asthmatics in Year Eleven, who've spent time in oxygen bubbles gasping for grim life, who race past me in cross-country. I am a rubbish runner.'

'I've made you really sad now, haven't I?' she said.

'No, it's fine, I needed to know. I'd rather hear this from you.' I sighed. 'So you've been telling people it's not true?'

'Of course I have, Poppet,' Vixen said. 'But you know what Blitzen is like. She really is beastly, isn't she?'

'Hmmm,' I said. I'd no doubt in my mind that these rumours were mainly coming from Blitzen ruddy Trapper. I felt like running over to the Trapper mansion and jumping the security gates and dragging her out by her stupid peroxide hair, even if there was a strong chance I'd get eaten by those three enormous Rottweilers who roam the grounds hospitalizing innocent people who trespass without permission.

'Are your parents still hopping mad?' Vixen said. Your mother told my mother that you're grounded and not allowed any guests. She meant me. Oh gosh, Popz, things are so quiet without you. I went out with Felix last night to a book launch but he brought his new girlfriend Coco, so it was a bit, erm, odd.'

'What is she like?' I said.

'Oh she's fine,' said Vixen, 'totally fine. Very pretty. Massively quiet though. I don't quite get them as a couple. She doesn't really say anything. Oh well, she said something about liking scented candles. Or not liking them. I can't remember. I think he's just with her for her looks.'

'Hmmm I see,' I said.

'I need you back on the social scene *tout de suite*, Popz, like is DULL without you. Can't you convince your mother you've learned your lesson?'

'I think I have learned my lesson,' I said. 'I know there's hardly any point lying to them as they always find out. And I know I'm not going to get away with not knuckling down at Lycée. In fact I've been actually quite enjoying my English work. Kitten's been coaching me and we've had quite good fun. Fat lot of good that is though, because I'm still grounded, spending all weekend helping Knute dig a chicken pen in the garden.

And moneywise I'm living off spare coppers I've cleaned out from down the back of the sofas.'

'What, no money at all?' gasped Vixen.

'Vix, I had to put in a request yesterday to Kitten to buy me a box of tampons. I'm in hell, Vix. HELL.'

'Well you need to prove you've changed!' she said. 'It's all about the big gesture now, isn't it? You need to prove you want to be a different, better person.'

'How?' I said.

'Well I have an idea,' Vixen said. 'I was reading about the perfect thing today online. I know something that we could all do that would be a true voyage of discovery and personal growth! I'm going to speak to Daddy about it this afternoon and then I'll explain. Gosh I'm excited already.'

'What is it? Hang on, Vixen you don't need self-improvement,' I said. 'No one thinks you're pregnant with your second child.'

'Oh Popz, I do,' she said. 'I want my whole life to be one long journey of self-improvement. Take for example this afternoon, when I'll be perfecting the swirl icing on cupcakes with a view towards launching my own cupcake boutique – Vixen's Sugarspun Visions – within the next two years.'

'Vixen,' I said, 'you can't bake. I've never even seen you boil an egg.'

'I *couldn't* bake,' she said, 'but over the past weeks I've taken a cookery course and got Daddy to buy me a Magimix blender and now I'm really rather good. I'm going to nip off and bake a box of "Hooray! Popz Has Got Her Phone Back" cupcakes, right now. This is what I mean about my life being one long journey of self-improvement!' she said. 'I'll call you, byeeeeee.'

THURSDAY 18TH FEBRUARY

When the doorbell chimed I ran as fast as I could down the spiral staircase. Mummy wasn't home, she was with Flash at Mensa head office, pleading his case to be allowed back to junior club. Kitten was at her Narcotics Anonymous meeting and Mrs Minsk was taking tea with her friend Betty at Claridges, and Daddy and Knute weren't even in the country. I was completely alone.

I skipped down the corridor to the front door, checking the CCTV monitor, yelping in delight like a highly-strung Pomeranian and flinging open the front door.

'Duchess,' my boyfriend said.

'Kwame!' I grabbed him by the hand and dragged him in through the door and slammed it behind us. We both started giggling and trying to tickle each other and then I said, 'There's no one here, Kwame, everyone is out.'

'Really? Oh my gosh.' Kwame raised one eyebrow in a naughty way as if his mind was racing with all the furiously forbidden things we could be getting up to.

And then I pushed him up against the hallway wall and

we snogged underneath the partially destroyed antique Russian chandelier, which still has a cricket ball stuck in it.

This was awfully bold of me. In comparison to my friends I can be a bit, well, frigid, but something mad was happening in my brain and the snog went on for absolutely ages and I was pushing my hands up the back of his jumper and touching Kwame's lovely toned back and he had his hands on my bum and was nibbling my neck and I was thinking: Crikey Kwame, don't leave a mark or I'll be in worse trouble than before. And then just as I was beginning to think: Wow, Mummy, this was the best plan ever getting Kwame around here to be my tutor, I'm having the most fun I can possibly imagine having within this lifetime! Kwame suddenly took his hands off me, looked at his watch and said, 'OK, enough of this, we need to get on.'

'Pardon?' I stood there with my hair all messed up where he'd been running his hands through it and my cardigan pulled off my shoulder.

'Biology,' he said. 'Your GCSE revision. We need to make a start.'

'Kwame,' I sighed. 'You're kidding, I hope? I'm never going to pass GCSE Biology. I'm an idiot at science.'

'Don't be stupid,' he said.

'No, Kwame, I *am* stupid,' I said, feeling a touch silly stood there having been dropped mid-snog in favour of the biology textbook, which he was now pulling out of his satchel.

'You're not stupid, Poppet,' he said. 'You just don't apply yourself to your lessons. It just takes a bit of focus and determination, doesn't it?'

I stared at him. He sounded exactly like Miss Cathcart and, every respect to Miss Cathcart, but she is not someone I wish to associate with feeling my bum cheeks and nibbling my neck. In fact, that vision makes me enormously queasy.

'Where can we go and work?' he said.

'Erm, in the kitchen I suppose,' I said, unenthusiastically. 'There's a long table in there.'

'That sounds perfect,' he said. 'I've brought my fold-out posters of receptors and effectors. And one with all the central nervous system on it too. The CNS can be a tricky thing to get your head round.'

'Fantastiche,' I said, dryly, pointing towards the last door down the corridor.

'Downstairs?' he said. 'OK, I'll start getting set up then. Are you putting the kettle on?'

'Whatever for?' I said.

'Errrrm . . . a cup of coffee?' Something like that?'

My face must have clouded over.

'Oh, it's Mrs Minsk's day off,' I said, which I thought was a perfectly all-encompassing response, but Kwame looked puzzled.

'Who?' he said.

'Our housekeeper lady,' I said. 'Well, sort of family friend who lives with us.'

I never know how to describe Mrs Minsk, as she's been with our family longer than I've been alive, so saying 'housekeeper' out loud always feels a bit odd. According to Blitzen Trapper, I shouldn't feel like that, because deeming the staff as 'friends' is enormously vulgar. Blitzen's family only communicate with theirs via Post-it notes. I'm glad my family aren't like the Trappers.

'So, it's Mrs Minsk's day off?' Kwame said.

'Yes,' I said. 'I'm not really completely sure how I would make coffee. It's all sorts of pots and jugs and filters and stuff isn't it? We could call Starbucks and have them deliver?'

Kwame looked at me and shook his head. I'm sure he was trying not to laugh.

'I'll make the coffee,' he said.

'Really? Gosh you are clever.' I smiled, embarrassed.

We walked downstairs into the basement, which was all neat and freshly scrubbed as Mrs Minsk never leaves a single crumb out of place before her day off and there had been no time to mess it up again. Kwame stood in the centre of the room and spun round in a circle slowly.

'Jeeeeez,' he said. 'This kitchen is bigger than my mother's entire flat.'

'Gosh, I know, it's ridiculous, isn't it?' I said. 'It used to be three rooms down here and a big smelly boiler room but Mummy had that all taken away and the rooms knocked through into one and then made that back wall glass so now we can see into the garden and Knute can have his compost heap and his vegetable patch.'

Kwame didn't say anything, but I could tell he was thinking deeply.

'It's much better this way,' I said, filling the silence. 'The rooms down here were quite grotty anyway and terribly noisy because of the boiler. They'd been servants' quarters for like a hundred years.'

Kwame looked at me. I was feeling a bit self-conscious.

'Oh, we didn't make Mrs Minsk live in the basement with all the clanking of the boiler,' I said quickly. 'Mrs Minsk has a really charming little apartment on the first floor. Like a Granny Flat. Except, um, she's not my granny.'

Kwame began taking books out and placing them neatly on the table.

'I mean, it's just she feels more like my granny than my granny sometimes,' I wittered on. 'It's, sort of, complicated . . .' My garbling voice trailed off like a deflating party balloon.

'I see,' said Kwame.

My brain was scrambling trying to remember if Mrs Minsk ever lived in one of the rooms downstairs when they were grotty and noisy and we still called them 'the servants' quarters'. I think maybe she did at some point but it was a long time ago when I was very tiny. I definitely remember her taking me to the park and to ballet and sleeping here. But where? Mummy had her textile studio on the first floor back then as I used to love to sneak up there and play with the paint. Did that mean Mrs Minsk was sleeping downstairs? However did she get to sleep with the boiler banging and giving off stinking smells? I tried to shut my brain off.

In the meantime, Kwame had filled the kettle with water and switched it on, then found one of those cafetiere pots that Daddy is always faffing about with. Kwame opened the cupboard closest to the kettle and took out coffee and began spooning the brown powder into the pot.

'There's about five different bags open, so I'm just using this Fair Trade one if that's OK?' he said.

'Super,' I said. 'Wow! How did you learn to do that?'

'What, make coffee? I worked in the Worcester Hotel in Edgware, back in the day,' he said. 'I used to make up the room-service trays orders.'

I stared at him. There are so many parts of his life I had no idea about.

'I loved that job,' Kwame said. 'And they paid me cash-in-hand, but they let me go after about ten shifts.'

'Why?' I said.

'They worked out I was only thirteen.' I told them I was seventeen. I had a little bit of stubble on my top lip and I coloured it in with a felt-tip pen to make it look like a proper moustache. And I fooled them when I went for the interview with the head chef, but it was really hot in the kitchen so the moustache kept rubbing off. And the ink kept staining my teeth.'

Kwame started laughing and I tried to, too, but on the table lay a pile of books with complicated names like *CNS Explained: 1.0* and *Biology: the Key to Life.* They were beginning to make me feel increasingly tense. Kwame brought the tray of coffee across and then he plunged the lever on the top of the coffee pot down.

'So what do you know about the central nervous system?' he said.

'Well, it's, um, that thing, erm, inside you,' I said, vaguely. 'The thing that sends all the messages to the, erm, bits of the body about stuff, isn't it?'

'Yes.' Kwame nodded. 'And how does it do that?'

I could feel my face getting hot now.

'Well, there's thingumywotists in your ears and eyes and nose and stuff, aren't there?' I said quietly. 'And they change when they come into contact with stuff, don't they?'

'Do you mean receptors in your sense organs, which detect stimuli in the environment?' Kwame asked calmly.

'Yes, that's exactly what I meant,' I said, feeling my ears slightly sizzle with humiliation.

'OK, well why don't you write that down?' Kwame told me.

I opened my pencil case with a loud, cross, zip of the zip, which Kwame took no notice of, took out a black fine ink-pen, opened my notebook and wrote some words down on a page in block capitals, which I hoped signified my huge annoyance.

'Brilliant,' said Kwame. 'OK, so now let's think about the different sense organs and what these receptors might be sensitive to.'

At that precise moment, inside my head, I could almost hear my mother laughing loudly like a rabid seagull. Kwame had been in the house less than thirty-five minutes, and instead of snogging him all I wanted him to do was leave. He was deadly serious about completing his day's tutorial and didn't seem to be remotely interested in snogging, canoodling, groping, nibbling, licking or any other sorts of nefarious behaviour that would cheer this bleak biology lesson up.

In fact, we worked seriously for another thirty-five, very long, minutes with me trying not to lose my temper and stay focused on the job at hand, until finally, I heard a rumpus in the corridor upstairs and Flash's voice saying, 'But we both know Guinevere is a God-bothering weirdo really, don't we Mummy?'

And Mummy saying, 'Flash, for Heaven's sake! I've just gifted the head of Mensa a very fine antique vase to help convince him you'll stop saying things like that. She's a CREATIONIST, not a weirdo.'

'So can I not say God-bothering Creationist?' Flash said. 'Why would God mind if he was being bothered if it was by someone who believed in him? I don't think that's a bad thing to say?' Then he tumbled down the stairs shouting, 'Mummy, has Mrs Minsk bought any more strawberry milk?' before spotting us and his eyes went very wide and his mouth dropped open and he ran back up the stairs shouting, 'Poppet is in the kitchen with someone and I don't know who it is and he's a black person. Mummy, come and look!'

'Oh, Flash, for God's sake,' I muttered, wishing he'd get past the stage of saying exactly what he thinks the moment he thinks it, then sadly accepting that our whole family are like that and Granny is still doing it and she's in her ruddy eighties.

'It's fine,' Kwame said, laughing, examining his arms and hands and saying, 'Hang on, Poppet, you never told me I was black! When were you going to get round to telling me?'

I nodded slowly at him and said, 'Kwame, you're black. Well you're more brown really. I was waiting for the right moment.'

Then we heard Mummy shouting, 'Flash, that's Kwame, darling. Go and say, "Hello Kwame", and stop being a silly sausage. Kwame knows all about science. You could ask him about that Large Hadron Collider thing you keep talking about.'

Flash ran back down the stairs and looked at Kwame and said, 'Hello, Cammby! Do you know anything about the Large Hadron Collider? What do you think will happen if they find the Higgs Boson particle? Will the world change for ever?'

Well Kwame's face really perked up then as if his brain was sparking to life and finally being used for something a bit intellectual.

'That's an excellent question, little man.' And then Kwame began talking about some bonkers scientific machine in Switzerland called the LHC, which I've never even heard of, which has tubes shooting all over the place and hundreds of scientists all working day and night for years to figure out how to bash a particle beam into another particle beam, which they hope one day will uncover the mystery of life. Or something like that, anyway. It was all jolly flummoxing.

'I don't understand the point though,' I butted in. 'Why would they spend so long bashing things into other things to find what's there?'

'Because, Poppet,' said Flash, sympathetic to my dimness, 'no one knows what is smaller than the particles they're crashing together. So if they can find out what that substance is, we can find out the origins of Planet Earth!'

'Yes.' Kwame nodded. 'That's totally right.'

Well then Flash clambered on to a chair and the pair chatted about this collider thing for about twenty more minutes and then Kwame said he had to rush off as he was meeting his A-level revision group at the British Library.

'See you, Flash,' he said. 'I'll send some links to Poppet that she can pass on about all the conspiracy theories about the LHC, they'll make you laugh.'

Kwame left without even kissing me goodbye, he just

ruffled my hair and said, 'I'll text you later.'

As the front door closed I sat in the kitchen surrounded by pieces of ruddy annoying A4 paper covered in drawings of ears and noses and nerves while Flash slurped his strawberry milk saying things like, 'I like Kwame, Poppet! He's amazing!' and then 'He's the best tutor we've ever had here!'

'He's not a tutor, Flash,' I said, grumpily. 'He's my *boyfriend*.'

'Haha, yes, OK,' said Flash, clearly humouring me. He wandered upstairs, still giggling at the very notion.

SUNDAY 21ST FEBRUARY

Newsflash: Striker Earhart is back in Octavia Square. I'm sure the entire square knows by now. In fact, there are deaf people in adjacent postcodes who know about it. I'm surprised *Sky News* aren't leading on it.

I was first made aware of Striker's reappearance into public life at about ten p.m. last night when my phone rang with an unknown number about four times in a row. I never, ever, ever, pick up unknown numbers. Like, duh, who does? It's usually a prank call from one of the goons from Godspeed Academy shouting, 'BARBED-WIRE GOB', or some weirdo trying to get you to swap mobile phone insurance packages. But when it rang the fifth time I had to pick it up out of sheer nosiness.

'Poppet?' a voice shouted. 'Poppet?! I'm at Stanstead

Airport. I'll be home in an hour, I'm on a payphone as my phone has been smashed by a mad woman. Ugh, God this handset smells vile. I've probably caught Herpes Type One or something.'

'Striker,' I said, 'are you by yourself?'

'No, I'm not,' she said, 'but I'm ruddy going to be soon. Orphelia is still stalking me. Look, Poppet, watch out for me coming. We need to speak as soon as possible. This is a ruddy Code Red. DON'T AGREE TO ANYTHING AN ADULT TELLS YOU, RIGHT? Say no to everything.'

'What are you talking about?' I said, feeling anxious.

'And Vixen too!' Striker shouted. 'Ignore her! I think they've brainwashed her to work for the other side. Or she's been cloned and her evil twin has been employed to destroy us. I can't tell which yet.'

'Striker, stop freaking me out,' I tutted. 'What's Vixen done?'

'I'll be home in an hour,' Striker said. 'Remain calm and indoors and don't agree to anything your parents tell you.'

By this point I'd decided I wasn't in the mood to be part of another one of Striker's hysterical fits.

'Striker,' I said, firmly, 'I'm here with Kitten and she's asleep on the sofa. My parents aren't here. Have you been eating paranoid pills? No one is trying to force me to do anything.'

'Where are they?' Striker said.

'Daddy is in New York and Mummy's gone to the opera in Covent Garden with Vixen's mother and . . . oh, your mum too.'

'Exactly,' Striker said, 'they're all out together, aren't they?'

'Well, yes . . . but I mean, they sometimes do, don't they?' I said. I was starting to get her point, 'Oh hell . . . what are they planning?'

'All will be revealed,' Striker said. 'And I'll tell you something, Popz, we're not going down without a fight. Oh damn, here's Orphelia,' Striker said. Her hand went over the phone receiver but I heard a muffled, 'Yes, Orphelia! Yes! You can leave me alone now, thank you. Yes, I'm OK to get myself home. NO need to come with me. Oh you're coming anyway? That's nice! Hang on, hark, what's that I hear? Is that the pilot revving up your return flight to SwitzBOREland. Oh, you're not listening to me as usual. *Quel surprise!*'

And in the midst of this rant the phone went dead.

I walked at a brisk, slightly rattled pace up the fifth-floor TV den where Kitten was snuggled in a foetal position on the sofa. She had a pale-blue Pashmina shawl wrapped around her and her head on a cushion and her mouth slightly open. Kitten is training for a fifteen-kilometre charity run at the moment so she's always up at half-five padding the streets of Hampstead in lycra tights before zonking out asleep before nine p.m. with her phone switched off. This is a good way to ensure none of her old drug-taking buddies can call her and tempt her to go out and get smashed.

'Kitten,' I said, standing over her with my hands on my hips. 'Kitten, can you hear me? Are you awake?'

Kitten didn't move, but then she said in a completely deadpan manner, 'I am now, you hideous brat. Has the DVD started?'

'The DVD has finished, Kitten,' I told her. 'You started making a noise like a pig during the opening scenes.'

Kitten still hadn't opened her eyes.

'Do you know about some sort of plan Mummy has in store for me?' I said. 'Something about Striker and Vixen.'

There was a long silence. Kitten rearranged her lips now as if she was crossing the borders back to snoozeworld and couldn't hear me. But there's a good reason why Kitten never made it as an actress, despite the thousands of pounds Mummy poured into acting classes and showreels and flying her First Class to Los Angeles to meet with important A-list agents. It's that Kitten has no natural acting ability whatsoever.

'Kitten, what do you know?' I said. I moved forward, gently picking up her right eyelid and lifting the skin. One bare, veiny eyeball peered back at me.

'Ow, get off!' she moaned, pushing me away. 'I don't know anything.'

'LIAR.'

'I don't! I've got better things to do than stick my nose

into yours and Mummy's relationship. I don't know what's going on.' She rolled over to face the back of the sofa, pulling her Pashmina over her face so I couldn't inflict any further eye-torture.

'Pah!' I laughed. 'Kitten, you know everything about this house. You and Voychek Potato Head should, like, totally get married and have little spy babies with beaky noses and sonic-range ears and binocular eyeballs. Tell me what you know.'

Kitten yelped as I prodded her back with my finger. 'I don't know . . . aghh . . . GET OFF! I don't know anything really!'

'What do you mean *really*?' I said. 'What *really* bit do you *nearly* know?'

'OK, OK, OK, OK! Get off me you total tit!' she shouted, sitting up. 'Right, don't have a crap-attack! And I didn't tell you, right?'

'Tell me what?'

'They're sending you to bootcamp,' she said, wincing.

'I BEG YOUR PARDON!'

'See, I knew you'd flip out,' she said.

I towered over Kitten, pulling a face like an angry bull who'd just spotted an idiot rambler crossing his field. 'Bootcamp?' I hissed.

'Well, OK, it's not so much bootcamp,' she said. 'More like a high-impact, self-assesment, um, personality-realigment course. I think you're allowed to come home at night . . . but then you have to go back . . . erm, quite a few times. It's called Fresh Start Foundation.'

This verbose description didn't make it sound any better. Two furious snorts of hot air shot down both my nostrils.

I didn't like the sound of a 'fresh start'. I don't think I need to be rebooted like a malfunctioning computer. I'm not even that bad.

'Fresh has been getting lots of press attention recently,' Kitten said, sitting up. 'Lots of Hampstead and Chelsea families are using it on their wayward kids. Everyone thinks it's the answer. Do you remember when Sincere McGarry, my friend Jonquella's little sister disappeared off to America before Christmas? With that pro skateboarder guy with the turquoise hair she met on Facebook?'

'Yes,' I said. Everyone remembers that. All those pictures of her turned up on her Facebook page, with a tattoo of daisy chains right up her stomach and she was in the bath showing her bits and it was totally embarrassing and Jonquella's mother was going, like, totally ape threatening to take her inheritance off her. And the McGarry's own three hundred hotels and a sky scraper in Dubai, so Sincere McGarry had SERIOUSLY messed up.

'Well she's been on Fresh Start Foundation since then,' Kitten said. 'It's suppose to make you think about life. It's cleaning up river banks, scrubbing grafitti, that sort of thing.'

This was getting ludicrous.

'Kitten, I'm nothing like Sincere McGarry!' I huffed.

'Sincere McGarry had her tongue cut in half in Las Vegas and it's in two horrible wobbly strips. Sincere McGarry was thrown out of the Scientology religion for making THEM look weird. That was by the Scientologists, for crying out loud. Kitten, you've got to sort this out, this is all your ruddy fault.'

'It's not my fault! I told Mummy to cut you some slack, but Paloma Earhart and Ramona Diaz-Brocklehurst are all really into it. They think it's the answer to all their problems.'

'Kitten,' I said. 'You spent the last five years out of your mind on Class As and now I'm being ruddy sent to bootcamp for having a fag behind the school, as Mother thinks I'm turning into you. This is ALL your fault.'

'Look, Popz,' said Kitten, cringing guiltily at my last sentence, 'I know what you're saying but if you want to blame anyone, blame Vixen Diaz-Brocklehurst. She came up with this idea! She read about the course and emailed the weblink to Paloma Earhart. Vixen suggested that you all enrol for it. OK, I didn't want to tell you that but there, I said it, deal with that.'

Kitten did a little 'suck that up' smile then grabbed the TV Sky+ controls and flipped to Paramount Comedy Network and started watching *Everybody Loves Raymond* intently like it was her favourite ever show in the whole world and I was spoiling it.

'I don't believe you!' I said. 'Vixen would never be so stupid as to . . . oh . . . *oh God.*'

My sentence ended abruptly.

Vixen certainly was feasibly stupid enough to have suggested Striker, her and myself enrol for 'a behavioural re-alignment and task-orientated five-part self-analysis workshop', featuring tasks such as trudging the streets at three a.m. poking collapsed tramps in doorways to check they're breathing, scrubbing bird crap and grafitti off the side of London Underground trains and performing Broadway musical numbers in old folks' homes. (Holy crap, if anything will convince oldies they'd be in a far cheerier position dead it's an hour of watching trust fund kids tunelessly wailing and pulling extreme jazz hands.)

But, of course, this is exactly the type of thing Vixen would find enormously spiritually nourishing. And of course, Ramona, her mother, would think so too. If Vixen was scrubbing the grafitti off an underpass and hugging the homeless she wouldn't have time to drain money out of her trust fund and wire it directly to Argentina to her save the Street Cats foundation.

On appearing back in 1 Octavia Square it was apparent that Striker did NOT share Vixen's philanthropic world view. It was an unusually warm February night and I stood on the doorstep waiting to see her, earwigging on dinner-party noises blaring from house windows and watching the paperazzi mopeds buzzing like mosquitos around the square, hoping to catch one of our neighbours' celebrity friends looking remotely tipsy *en route* home so they could whizz the photo onto websites for the whole world to disapprove of.

I was also feeling oddly discombobulated by Felix's attic room light, which was on, meaning he was at home. I stared crossly at the attic window, wanting to call him right there and tell him I needed him and his friendship and he had to stop whatever fun he was having in there with his new friend Coco. Then I told myself not to be silly, and he wouldn't be having fun with Coco anyway as she was stupid and about as deep as an egg-cup. And I bet she never made him laugh so much he nearly choked on a chocolate digestive and well, whatever, I didn't care anyway, I hoped they were happy and I hoped her allergy to the dust in the house was fine and hadn't choked her.

Safe to say, I was in a pretty odd mood.

And then Striker arrived, making a spectacular entrance, attempting to exit a people carrier still moving at five miles per hour as the driver cruised slowly round the square looking for her front door.

'I'm getting out here, Orphelia,' Striker was saying firmly. 'I'm not going in that bloody house. I'm going to stay at Poppet's. Tell Mother I can be visited by appointment only and I have no forseeable appointments at this present juncture. Goodbye, Orphelia, you twisted old womble!'

Orphelia barked back in her mightly exasperated American accent, which had suddenly lost all its Californian chilled-out vibe, 'Striker, will you hold steady!

We are still in transit! You are going into your own house, young lady. I told your mother I'd deliver you home and DAMMIT TO HIGH HEAVEN that's what I'll achieve. And then, young lady, you're on you're on your own. I don't ever want to set eyes on you ever again, you ungrateful godforsaken creature! It's a wonder I've not strangled you by now!'

These didn't sound like the words of an eminent child-psychologist at all. I've seen Dr Orphelia Lovell's books for sale in airports all over the word with titles like, *Understanding Teenagers: Love Will Save the Day*, and, *Zen ways to Tame Your Teen*, and at no point did she ever seem like someone who'd threaten to physically assault her patients. But it was safe to say that Orphelia was possibly at the end of her tolerance having travelled across Europe in charge of a peroxide-haired Tazmanian Devil in blood-red lipstick and patent leather snakeskin stilettos. Striker, indeed, still looked marvellous, and bang-on *Teen Vogue* autumn/winter trend despite having been imprisoned for ten days up the side of a mountain.

'Poppet!' Striker shouted. 'I'm coming to stay with you, indefinitely. I'll have the driver bring my bags.'

By this point two paparazzi guys had leaped off their mopeds and were snapping pics of Striker and then of me stood there in my long, grey towelling Sith Lord hooded dressing-gown and patchwork moccasin slippers. They've spent years filming Kitten and her friends and ignoring us as we were just little kids going to boring kiddy parties, but now we're valuable to them too.

'Hello, Striker Earhart,' one of the paps shouted to her. 'What's happening here, then? More drama?'

'Oh, go away,' said Striker, although she was slighly posing for a picture at the same time.

I hate it when the paps do this. You have to remember, they're not simply photographing you, they're videotaping you too. They need you to speak so they can put the little scene up online. People all over the world love watching you looking annoyed and uncomfortable about the horrid things the paps say. The more you tell the pap filming to leave you alone, the better the clip becomes and the more money it's worth, so the very best thing to do is say nothing at all. If only Striker would learn that, or be a little less pleased that they knew her name.

'Striker,' I said, 'shhhh.'

'Ha!' laughed the second pap. 'Here's me thinking you little rich girls live the life of luxury, but there's always a drama isn't there? Which one of you is pregnant by that gangster?'

Striker's face crumpled. 'I'm not pregnant!' she said.

'Oh ignore him, he means me,' I mumbled. They'd clearly had a tip-off from someone at Hampstead Lycée about that rumour. I *wonder* who could have done that?

'Can you leave us alone please?' I said, covering my face with my hand. 'I'm not giving you permission to film us.'

'How's your sister, Poppet?' the first pap said. 'Still off

the booze? Or is she indoors passed out under a pile of bottles, business as usual?'

I took a deep breath to prevent myself lunging forward and karate-chopping him right in the windpipe and chucking his stupid camera in a bush, which would be a terrible idea as he'd sue my father for assault and then make him buy them a newer, bigger camera. Just then, out of the corner of my eye, Vixen appeared in view. 'Vixy!' I shouted. This was rather a surreal moment. I'd not set eyes on my friend for two weeks and here she was stood in the middle of the road wearing a pair of white cotton pyjamas and black velvet slippers, holding a plate of ridiculously delicious-looking cupcakes, which were about two centimentres of sponge and six centimentres of frosted cream and pink icing speckled in silver stars.

'Striker! Hooray! Welcome home! I made you cupcakes!' Vixen trilled.

Striker turned her head and glared at Vixen using an expression that could have turned Vix to stone.

'Welcome home?' Striker said. 'Welcome home? Oh yes, I feel so welcome here, Vixen, you ruddy blithering, hippy-dippy-save-the-ruddy-poorly-pawed-squirrel-let's-mess-up-everyone's-life-for-them-as-my-three-good-braincells-clearly-overloaded-weeks-ago-utter-NINCOMPOOP!'

'Oh . . . oh, come on, Striker,' I said. 'That's not nice.'

'Nice!' shouted Striker. 'She gone and signed us all up

for a weird brain-reprogramming bootcamp!'

Well, Vixen's face curdled like she might begin to weep, but then she pulled her shoulders back and retorted, 'Listen, Striker Earhart. Why don't you just button up your big, snapping trap for once in your ridiculous life? Poppet's been grounded for weeks because of you! I'm trying to help!'

'Help? How is this a help?' Striker said.

'Well, *excusez-moi si'il vous plait* for coming up with a plan to make your mother respect you again! I must apologize for finding a way for Poppet's mother to stop disinheriting her of millions of pounds! Oh naughty, evil Vixen! I'm the bad one here! Naughty, naughty me!'

'OH, SHUT UP, VIXEN,' shouted Striker, 'you're not my mother. Shut up.'

'Ha! Me shut up?' gasped Vixen. At this juncture I thought Vixen may finally flip and, going against three years of after-school transcendental meditation classes, chuck a teacup at Striker's head. 'YOU shut up, Striker! The entire Square, the whole of Hampstead, the entire world is bored to ruddy death with you!'

Well, what happened after this point, I'm trying to put from my mind. However, if ever I want to relive Striker and Vixen's big screaming argument, in full technicolour, web 2.0 quality, accompanied by six hundred and seventy-eight bitchy comments on the comment box, they should go to the archive section at www.CelebInferno.tv where it's preserved in time for ever.

* * *

Striker didn't sleep in her own house last night. She won that little battle at least. She's lying in my bed right now, fast asleep with eye make-up all over her face. I'm on my sofa with a duvet. We didn't get to sleep till four a.m. as we were both quite shaken up. I must record here for posterity that Striker had a little weep when she got back here and said she was very sorry about everything that has happened, what with me getting grounded and Hampstead Lycée girls saying I was pregnant and me now being completely poor and driven around by Voychek and tutored on the central nervous system by my boyfriend for a hundred and fifty pounds a week, which was so 'random and wrong' she didn't even know where to begin.

Striker lay on her side on my bed and wept, saying that this was all a mess and she didn't know how things could have gone so terribly wrong. I gave her a cuddle and told her everything was going to be fine and we'd sort it all out.

All I have to do now is work out how.

MONDAY 22ND FEBRUARY

I blame Flash for today.

I'd almost, well nearly almost, cajoled Mummy around to my way of thinking about Fresh Start Foundation. I'd been working hard for twenty-four hours to get her thinking this whole thing was a beastly, damaging affair, a massive waste of money (IT COSTS twenty thousand pounds AND SHE'S TAKING IT OUT OF MY TRUST FUND) plus a terrible way to spend my half-term holidays, especially when I could be helping her source tiles for her new design project and having lunch with her in Harvey Nichols, enjoying some some 'girls' time together' over a plate of yummy lobster spaghetti. (It says a lot about any teenager's social diary when hanging about with her mother is the better option than what she has planned.)

I could see that whole 'girls' time' line, which I delivered to her last night as she said goodnight, had tweaked Mummy's heart strings, as her lip wobbled when I said it, like she wanted this more than anything in the world.

So, thank you, Flash. I was *this close* to a day browsing peacock feather and rare gemstone hair accessories in Fenwicks in Bond Street while mother faffed around trying on hats, but instead I spent the day in hell.

Ruddy Flash and his Montague-Jones family tree project. Lorks o' Lordy, how I wish I'd never encouraged him with that silly ruddy thing. It was unsettling enough when he found out that Granny and her friends basically drained a Zambian emerald mine dry, *which wasn't even officially theirs,* in the 1950s, by charming a Zambian village chief into signing all sorts of weird paperwork he didn't understand, but then I find out that I own the emeralds. They're in a vault in my name. I own almost 5.2 million pounds worth of emeralds that never belonged to our family in the first place, and apparently the place in Zambia they're from hasn't even got any schools or much clean running tap water. I've pictures of the blasted things now, and it turns out I could never go anywhere wearing them anyway as they're so enormous and garish I'd get mugged at gunpoint the second I stepped out of the Montague-Jones vault. And even if I did have one of those huge, 300lb security guards to follow me around Coutts Bank, or I went everywhere in a bulletproof glass box on wheels, bright green doesn't even suit me. So, yeah, sorry about that, Zambia. Sorry I stole millions of pounds of natural resources off you. Sorry about those pictures of the kids with flies all over their heads starving on the Africa Aid website, but Granny does like sparkly things.

Then, just as we come to terms with that, Flash starts looking into Great, Great, Great Grandfather Algernon in 1880 and it turns out he '*aided in the transportation of hundreds of West Africans to America, which greatly effected the landscape and development of Alabama*'.

Now, this sounds slightly noble doesn't it?

But then it turned out Algernon wasn't, in fact, a travel agent. No, the West Africans didn't have any ruddy choice but to go to America and help build it as they'd been forced on a ship by people with dogs and whips.

Now, I've tried really, very, very hard to think of this as

a positive thing, in the long run, as maybe it was nice for them to travel and see other places? And America is lovely. I mean, golly, when Vixen and I go to the Hamptons in summer we have an absolute blast. Lots of people on the Cottingham Estate don't even have passports – they'd love to go there. But no, there's no cheery spin on this, Great, Great, Great Grandfather Algernon was *trafficking slaves.* HOW MORTIFYING.

Flash found this out as he uncovered a letter to our solicitors from some jolly angry African-American people in Alabama, USA, saying they want Slave Labour Reparations i.e.: some money to compensate them for all the bits of America that were built for free by black people. I felt sick when Flash mentioned this and I emailed Mr Chenowitz and told him to give them all ruddy Zambian emeralds as by this point the blasted things just made me feel queasy. Mr Chenowitz said it wasn't as simple as that. He said I had to remember that twelve million people were 'convinced to leave Africa' over a period of three hundred years, so a few diamonds wouldn't really help much. This made me rather depressed and I had to have a serious word with Flash to never, ever, ever, ever, ever breath a word of this to Kwame or Dragon. Up to now Flash has blackmailed three Kinder eggs out of me in hush money.

So when Flash piped up this morning that he'd uncovered *another* branch of the Montague-Jones family tree, my response should have been, 'Really, Flash? Gosh is that the time? I need to go upstairs and rearrange my sock drawer into seasonal sections.' But no, like a buffoon, I said, 'Oh go on then, hit me with it. It can't get any worse.'

'Did you know that one of our relatives was banned from Buckingham Palace by Queen Victoria?' he said.

'What for?' I said, though Mummy had appeared in the kitchen and I should have tried double-hard to make him be quiet.

'For being a bad influence on the future heir to the throne and bringing the monarchy into disrepute!' Flash replied.

'Wonderful,' I said.

Flash then proceeded to tell me about our ancestor Lord Aubrey Jeremiah Montague who kicked around with all the A-list tier of Royals in the 1850s and was a totally infamous party-animal who gambled thousands of pounds at poker with Prince Bertie, the Queen's son, and wasted thousands more pounds on bottles and bottles of a painkilling drug called Laudanum and his favourite tipple, gin.

'What's syphilis, Poppet?' Flash asked me.

'Syphilis?' I said, almost choking on my porridge. 'Erm, well, it's a disease, Flash. A quite bad one.'

'Well it must be quite bad, Poppet, because Great, Great, Great, Great, Great, Great Grandfather Aubrey, who was banned from Buckingham Palace, died of it when he was thirty-seven. Although the doctors weren't sure if the disease killed him. It was more likely to be the booze he drank to forget about the disease.'

'Really?' I said, in a dry voice. 'Oh. Hooray! Another happy story. Flash that must be the fifth booze-related Montague family death you've told me about. Go Team Us!'

Flash ignored my sarcasm and carried on scribbling into his notebook.

'Hey, Flash, you should call the BBC and see if they want to make a documentary series about us. I'm so proud of all our ancestors. Instead of *Who Do You Think You Are?* they could call it *A Series of Terrible Depressing Tales About a Bunch of Alcoholic Slave-Trading Emerald Thieves*!'

'Do you think the BBC would be interested?' he said.

'NO! I mean, yes probably. Look I was joking. Don't call the BBC for God's sake! In fact, Flash, I've got a good mind to throw your family tree project and your ruddy Ancestors Uncovered software in the bin. It's driving me insane!'

'Don't you dare!' said Flash, narrowing his eyes like a venomous puff adder. 'Mummy, tell her! Tell Poppet she can't destroy history just because she doesn't agree with it.'

'Poppet, stop annoying Flash,' Mummy said, staring distractedly at her Blackberry. 'Why are you destroying history?'

'I'm not!' I said. 'Don't listen to him, Mummy. He's such a baby.'

'Poppet is cross,' said Flash, loudly, 'because I keep finding ancestors who've died of booze and drug overdoses and that sillyfish disease. She is in denial!'

'Flash, I beg your pardon,' Mummy said. 'How many of our ancestors have died of things like that?'

'Oh lots of them!' said Flash, thrilled someone was taking an interest. 'Would you like me to put together a Powerpoint presentation and show you?'

'Poppet,' Mother said, spinning her head round to me, 'get your bag and get into that car. You're late. You're going on that Fresh Start course. Why are you still here?'

'But Mummmmmy,' I said, 'what about our girls' time?'

'Oh, Poppet, that's so sweet,' Mummy said. 'When you've finished the course, we can have tons of it. Every single Saturday night until you're thirty-five if you want. Get in that car. Voychek has texted me twice asking where you are. You know how he hates to be off-schedule.'

'Flash, I hate you,' I said.

'Oh, bye bye Poo-Pop,' said Flash, waving his little hand. 'Good luck on your bootcamp! Historians will only have nice things to write about you! That would be awesome!'

I stormed to the car and got into the back seat, pulling my seatbelt across and placing my face against the window, before sitting for a while doing heavy breathing, to make my point that I really was jolly irate. Then I remembered Voychek couldn't give a holy flying poo whether I'm happy, mad, bad, sad or dying slowly of Polynesian Mombo Mombo Virus. All Voychek cares about is that he's on the right side of Mummy, who pays his wages. Voychek hadn't even noticed I'd got into the car, he was picking his nose so intently I was pained to interrupt.

'Are we picking up Striker and Vixen?' I said, curtly.

'Who?' he said, wiping his fingers on his trousers and starting the car engine.

I sighed. Who? Yes, Voychek. You can't remember them, can you? Damn your selective amnesia.

'Striker and Vixen,' I said again. 'My friends who live there and there on the square.' I pointed at their houses, then folded my arms.

'I not know them,' Voychek said. 'I have on my list that I just drive you to Hackney Wick. Just you. No other people.'

'But they live just THERE,' I said. 'Voy . . .'

But then I shut up. I hate to admit this but Voychek has completely broken my determination to conquer him. He's been so relentlessly difficult and unyieldingly pain-like-an-enormous-pulsating-boil-in-the-rear-end-ish that I see no point now even trying to fight. And the worst thing of all is, I think he knows it.

We left Octavia Square heading towards Hackney and with every metre we travelled I felt smaller and decreasingly feisty, sat there alone *en route* to some weird head-bending rehabilitation course, with neither of my best friends and fellow inmates to bolster me. I'd rung Striker and Vixen's phones repeatedly this morning but they were both on voicemail.

I wished now I'd taken this whole Fresh Start thing more seriously, but to be quite honest from the moment Kitten told me, I'd never really really truly thought it would happen. What were they going to do to me there? My throat began to feel tremendously cluttered with lumps and pieces of phlegm and my cheeks felt heavy, like I was about to break down and sob.

'Where is Hackney Wick, Voychek?' I said.

'East,' he said, tapping the side of his Tom Tom sat nav machine as if that explained everything.

'East?' I said. I've never really been anywhere in East London before. We live in North-west London and if we want to see chums we either go to a restaurant in Belgravia or Soho or we visit their houses in West London in Holland Park or Notting Hill. East London is somewhat of an enigma to me. When I got my first Oyster travel card last year I always intended to go and find Albert Square and have a mug of tea in Ian Beale's café and see the Queen Vic, but then it turned out that they weren't real people, it was a soap opera, and then the impetus to explore East London faded. Mummy says Spitalfields is quite charming these days, in a shabby-chic sense. Mummy met with the artist Tracy Emin in her gallery there last year and bought a couple of paintings from her and she said there were some delightful boutiques there and you could even get a decent Flat White coffee. I asked Voychek if this Hackney Wick place we were going was anything like Spitalfields and he snorted with laughter and said no.

We drove to Islington, past Angel Underground Station, then Highbury, and then onto a place called Clapton, where the place felt much poorer and the streets felt much narrower and the front doors and pavements much more neglected and all the shops were either boarded up or selling Dixie Chicken. Places like this don't freak me out as much as they used to, as the Cottingham Estate where Kwame lives is pretty rough, but then Voychek said something rather chilling.

'Murder Mile,' he said.

'What?' I said.

'Murder Mile. Nickname for this road. Lots of people shot dead here. Or stabbed.'

I stared out of the window. I could see no evidence of murders. In fact, the people seemed wholly unphased. They were wandering to work and waiting at bus-stops with totally normal, unterrified expressions. Being on a place called Murder Mile must have been quite normal. Well it wasn't for me! I didn't like it here one bit. I wanted to be back in Octavia Square in my lovely, warm, secure house with its double-thickness security windows and the safety room in the basement we've all been trained to run into and lock the doors if raiders ever manage to break in and try to kidnap us. I wanted to be in bed, watching my laptop under a twenty tog goose-feather duvet in a Heals organic-dyed duvet cover on my allergy-free pillow, hoping Mrs Minsk might be about to bake a nice plate of biscotti and see if I wanted to pop down for a mid-morning milky coffee and a chuckle at *The Archers* on Radio Four.

'Are we here yet?' I said, grumpily.

'No, we go further east,' he said, driving down side road after side road until we reached what felt like an abandoned industrial park. There was a row of miserable, forgotten factories, a car yard full of rusty scrap and, looking onto this, a site full of caravans with kids playing outside.

'Gypsies. Disgusting. They make mess,' said Voychek, pointing at the kids who were playing with a dog. They didn't seem to be disgusting. They seemed OK – in fact they were less scary than the kids in the Cottingham Estate, but Voychek seemed rather repulsed by them. I didn't know what to say. One of the kids caught my eye and waved cheekily at me. I quickly looked away. The car turned down a track which led down towards a canal.

'Here,' Voychek said, pointing at a Portacabin and picking up his phone, 'this must be it. I ring them, make sure.'

Voycheck dialled the number with his fat, mallet fingers then said, 'Yes, I got girl here. Poppet Montague-Jones. She here for, erm, bad girls' club.'

Voychek giggled at his own joke. 'Yes, all right, I know she late, I send her in now. Six p.m. finish, yes? Goodbye.'

The childlocks on the back door clunked and I jumped out, slamming my door with a defiant crash. Voychek just laughed. I know for a fact that the time I threatened to kick his back window out with my foot, he would have been overjoyed if I'd tried and shattered my ankle. Voychek finds my acts of minor rebellion uproariously amusing.

I trudged to the Portacabin's door and opened it nervously. The sight greeting me inside will stay with me for ever. At first all I saw was a sea of bright yellow. There were rows and rows of desks, and sat behind each one a person of around my age, clad in an insane acidic yellow boilersuit. I stood frozen to the spot. Some of the kids had their faces propped up on their hands, others had laid their faces on the desk and were dozing, others were staring forwards at the man at front lecturing them.

Then I heard a voice on the back row shout, 'Poppet!'

It was Striker! She was sat beside Vixen. They both smiled and waved. They seemed like they were on good terms, which was an enormous relief.

'Riiiiiight,' droned the man giving the lecture, turning to me. 'Well this isn't ideal, is it? Poppet – hang on, I've got your name down here. You're late. Do you realize that?' He had one of the most uninspiring, droning voices known within the human stratosphere, 'One of the key ideas here will be punctuality. If we say nine a.m., we mean nine a.m. on the dot. Not five past nine a.m. Not ten past nine a.m. We're trying to instill key ideas on fundamental life skills here. OK?'

'OK,' I said.

'OK. We'll provide you with your overalls when the talk is over,' he said. 'Now, can you sit down please? My name is Clarion McGrey and I'm your mentor today. I'm just talking about how Fresh Start gives individuals the chance to be introspective about your place in the cosmos and *chuntlyfunklysplunkywahwahpghghghggggwoom*.'

'OK, that's what it sounded like. I've no idea what he said to be honest as I zoned out soon after the words 'introspective about your place in the cosmos' as he was boring me senseless, plus I was too busy trying to see what Striker was signalling to me with her hands.

'Look,' Striker was mouthing, pointing with her finger at the end of the row, 'look who is here!'

'What?' I whispered back, possibly a little too loud. 'Oh. My. God.'

It was a remarkable vision. Sitting next to Vixen, on the end of the row, looking particularly silly in her banana-yellow 'bad girls' club' costume was my close personal friend Miss Blitzen Trapper. I let out a splutter of recognition. Blitzen glared at me, channelling pure poison.

'Hello, Blitzen!' I whispered and twinkled my fingers, feeling oddly brave now we were both on different unknown territory.

Blitzen Trapper was on the Fresh Start programme. My sister Kitten was completely right, all the richest familes were signing up for it.

But why Blitzen? I was absolutely dying to perch my bum on the side of Blitzen's desk right there and then and say, 'Blitz, come on 'fess up. What have you done?!'

Striker winked, picked up a pencil, scribbled something on a piece of paper, then passed it to me.

Stole Daddy's black Amex card. Bought Porsche Boxter. Let boyfriend drive it on Saturday night. He took it on M25 doing 100 mph and flipped it.

'Nooooooooo,' I said.

Half of me was buzzing on this delicious gossip and the other half was resentful that Blitzen Trapper was the only one of the four of us in Fresh Start club for something actually juicy. Suddenly shoplifting in Bodwin's Boutique seemed like something you might lose a Brownie Badge for. I checked Blitzen for any signs of car-wreck damage but she seemed in complete working order. Saying that, it was perfectly feasible that Blitzen could step from a flaming wreck utterly untouched, like a Satanic force in a horror movie.

'Was she in it?' I said to Striker.

'No, he'd just dropped her home, then he took it for a spin. He's in hospital. He's broken both his legs.'

'So today,' said Clarion McGrey, 'the point of the venture is to find a space of cleanliness inwardly in your soul by cleaning outwardly. This is also a chance to reconnect with nature.'

'Is he mentally ill?' I whispered to Striker.

'I think so,' she whispered back. 'But, like, y'know in a high funtioning way. Hang on.' Striker put her hand up.

'Yes, Striker?' he said.

'What are we doing today? I can't understand you,' she said.

'Well if you were listening and not chatting, you would understand,' he tutted. 'Can I remind you, Striker, that this is a learning-based unit accomplishment course?'

'What does that mean? I don't understand that either,' Striker sighed.

'It means,' he said, 'that if you fail to pass a unit, you will remain on the unit, completing it day after day until you've passed and are considered able to proceed. And your parents have signed forms saying they're happy with that. For some this is a very long road.'

'Oh,' said Striker.

'I missed what the unit is?' I said. 'What's the task?'

'We're cleaning the canal bankside,' said a boy with floppy, black emo hair shaven up the back.

'We're aiding,' butted in Clarion, 'in the regeneration of the Lea Valley nature area, so that future generations of Londoners can walk, jog, ride bikes and bring their families here.'

Well Blitzen Trapper seemed to find her voice now, which sounded rather aghast.

'Why in hell,' she began, 'do I care what happens over here in the Lea Valley conservation area? East London is a vile hell hole filled with hideous diseased peasants! I've got more inclination to book into the Elemis Day Spa in Helmand Province, Afghanistan, than ever come back here. Someone could gas them all for all I care.'

A Jewish-looking boy on the second row turned and peered as if he was hearing things. Clarion stared at Blitzen but he didn't seem ruffled. I was guessing by now that listening to spoiled brats moaning was his daily job.

Blitzen went on. 'I mean, seriously, have you looked at the state of things out there?' Blitzen fumed. 'It's just smashed-down ruddy factories and hideous muggle children playing with mongrel dogs, spreading headlice and fishing in a ruddy canal full of rotten algae and bikes.'

'Oh don't be horrid,' piped up Vixen. 'We're all the same under the skin. We're all God's creatures. Why don't you try to love more and stop being a hater?'

'All the same?' tutted Blitzen. 'I don't even share a basic DNA structure with the poor.'

Even Striker looked appalled at this. Striker can be feisty and spoiled sometimes, but she's not downright mean.

'Yes, Blitzen,' said Clarion, calmly, 'this is indeed a poor area, but it's being regenerated. And you're going to help.'

'But why should I help?' Blitzen asked.

'I think you might gain a lot from today, Blitzen,' smiled Clarion. 'OK, if everyone starts moving outside now, we can get to work. And will you all promise to take an extra-special look out for syringes? We've tried our very best to clear the area but I hear reports that one of the kids from the nearby traveller site managed to stand on one this week and she's having tests right now for Hepatitis C. Be careful out there.'

As the crowd began moving outdoors, a small hippy-type lady in a muddy walking boots, holding a clipboard, wearing a Gap hoodie over a floral smock and paisley leggings, took me to the side. She handed me a set of enormous yellow overalls and instructed me to put them on. I asked where the fitting room was and what size they were as they seemed XXL and I only take a Medium, but she simply feigned deafness and walked away. I turned my back on the group and pulled the shapeless baggy material over my skinny jeans and long T-shirt, then attempted to catch my reflection in the Portacabin window. It didn't work terribly well as a mirror, in fact all I could see was a big yellow lump like a depressed sun, frowning back.

'What the hell is Vulcron?' said Blitzen, who'd hooked one arm out of her boilersuit and was peering disgustedly at the washing label. 'It says here these overalls are twenty per cent Cotton, eighty per cent Vulcron!? Ugh. I've not heard of it. I very much doubt my mummy said it was OK for me to be seen in manmade fibres. Does anyone here have an anti-histamine pill if I come out in a rash. Clarion? If I have some sort of anaphylactic shock, I hope you have injections on hand or my father will sue you.'

Clarion just sighed, chivvying us all out of the door.

We began walking, down towards the canal path, then heading eastward on the path beside the water. Slightly smog-stained swans swam up to investigate us and a man in a canal boat brought his mug of tea outside then sat on the roof of his canal boat having a good long stare. There were about twenty of us in total. A balance of boys and girls. I was sure I recognized two boys as Charterhouse day-boarders that I met at the Westminster Abbey carol service last Christmas. One of the quietest members of the group I was pretty sure was a girl called Volka; a Russian oligarch's daughter I'd seen lots of times in the party pages in the *Evening Standard* Society section. She certainly didn't seem like she was in the party mood now. Striker, Vixen and I hung right at the back of the walking group, Blitzen walking a few metres ahead of us, not quite wanting to be friends with us, but sensing we were perhaps the safest option of not spending a day as Wilhemina-no-chums.

The path we were following was quite dirty and depressing. In some sections it was covered in dog mess, bird poo and slime. Clarion assured us this was all going to be cleared up and resurfaced and soon people in East London would have more places to get fresh air. Apparently some of this land had not been touched for hundreds and hundreds of years, and back then there was no rules where you could dump dangerous things like fluids and chemicals so the aim here was to 'decontaminate' then 'regenerate' the land.

'But there are people living here,' said Vixen. 'There're houses just there. And travellers living in caravanas. Have they been living in the middle of poison?'

'Well, yes,' Clarion said. 'But things are improving. Slowly. Anyway, we're nearly here!'

Around the next bend the path was blocked with scaffolding covered in plastic sheets. There was lots of red tape and a big sign telling pedestrians the path was closed and they needed to head for the main road.

Thank God, I thought, as I jolly well wanted away from this horrid place of muddy banks and depressing tower blocks and graffiti and the constant bird-poo ice-rink I was skidding about in. And now Clarion had begun saying that this piece of ground had been a tannery in Victorian times making leather goods, so builders and archaeologists had been digging up horses' skeletons and sharp knives and the smell had been terrible.

OK! I thought. You've made your point! It's grim. Can I go home now? But no, Clarion found a door in the tarpaulin and picked it up shouting, 'Hello? Douglas, we're here! I've another Fresh Start Group One for you.'

Then a man appeared with a beard only on his chin and no moustache or hair, who looked like his head was on upside down, wearing a *Brecon Beacon Nature Trail* T-shirt mumbling, 'Oh, oh right. Oh good, come through.'

Inside the tarpaulin, the sights and odours were pretty vile. This was the very worst part of the canal path, where people had spent years dumping rubbish and hanging about taking drugs, but now the plan was to turn it into a picnic ground.

'Have you ever watched that film *Hostel*?' Striker said. 'Y'know, the horror film where the backpackers book into that hideous torture den?'

'I hate horror films,' said Vixen, 'they give me anxiety for weeks.'

'This place reminds me of that film. There's something really creepy about it, isn't there? Isn't it amazing? It's like we're in a portal to hell. And we're Satan's slaves working here!' Striker laughed. It was the first time I'd seen her look really genuinely happy for ages. Striker grabbed a bin liner and some thick rubber gloves and was soon sifting through the mud to remove tin cans, children's toys, hair brushes, wine bottles and anything else that was classed as 'contamination'.

Meanwhile, I was watching with some satisfaction as Blitzen Trapper's face changed from pink, to pale, to white, to grey, to pale vomitous green.

'Are you having problems, Blitzen?' Clarion said, after twenty minutes, noticing she'd not managed to even put on her gloves or found a bag.

Blitzen didn't say anything. She simply folded her arms and made her mouth very small and tight like she was trying to stop a stream of angry words pour out.

'Blitzen, it's imperative that you join in with the task today,' said Clarion.

'I'm . . . I'm NOT doing it!' Blitzen finally snapped.

Striker started laughing.

'But Blitzen, I think it will be fun!' said Striker. 'Hey? What happens if we find a corpse, Clarion? Do you think anyone ever murdered anyone and buried them down here?'

Now, normally, I would find Striker's behaviour rather mean and unnecessary, but let's be honest, Blitzen does appear to have been rather busy recently causing havoc on my behalf, so I was enjoying her discomfort just a teensy-tiny touch.

'If I find a skull, or maybe the skeleton of a foetus, can I keep it?' shouted Striker. 'I'd like to put it in a jar in my bedroom. How amazing would that be. I love the grotesque!'

'Oh me too,' agreed Emo boy.

'I'm sure you can keep a foetus in a jar. That's not illegal,' said one of the Charterhouse boys. My godfather is a gynaecologist and he has one in his office.'

Blitzen was wilting fast. 'Shut up everyone!' she said. 'Clarion, I can't do this. I can't do filth. This mud. The dirt. I have a phobia. *I cannot.*'

'OK, Blitzen, BREATHE. Focus,' Clarion said. 'The others are winding you up. There's nothing terrible down here. We're just giving this patch a thorough check so that when the grass grows back there's no unpleasant surprises.'

'No. This. Is. Not. Possible,' she said. Blitzen's voice sounded rather robotic now, like she'd gone to an odd freaked-out head-space, 'I can't. I won't touch the mud. With my hands. I won't do it.'

'Oh, Blitzen, come on,' said Vixen, walking across and rubbing Blitzen's arm supportively. 'Yes you can. We're just tidying up! Don't you like tidying sometimes? I find it quite therapeutic. Somedays I tell our maid to put her feet up and I plug in my iPod and let the house flood with whale sounds, then I tidy my own bedroom! I think de-cluttering really frees up the mind and leaves more space for positivity.'

Blitzen shook Vixen off like she was a crackhead trying to mug her and said, 'Get off me. Are you insane? I don't tidy my room. I don't even let my own bath water out. I won't put my hand back in that vile water with all the muck in it.'

'It's your muck!' laughed Striker.

'The staff deal with muck,' Blitzen said. 'It's like emptying the bathroom bins of bathroom floss and tissue. Or picking up thongs off the floor. I don't do mess. END OF STORY. It's not my thing. It gives me the shivers.'

'Oh, like a proper medical condition?' said Vixen, still sounding sympathetic.

'I don't care what you call it,' Blitzen said.

'OK then,' said Vixen, undeterred, 'well that can be

your goal for today! To learn to love mud. That's exciting.'

Obviously, that wasn't the end of that. Following at least thirty more minutes of Blitzen Trapper whining and complaining and pretending to almost vomit and telling everyone she was about to faint, eventually Clarion put Blitzen in charge of carrying bin liners from the site to the van. It felt like he was backing down to her, but to be quite frank Clarion could have strangled Blitzen with his bare hands and thrown her still-twitching corpse into the canal by this point and he'd have got a loud round of applause.

Once Blitzen had stopped being so hideously aggravating, I decided to knuckle down and do some enthusiastic decontamination. I wanted to complete this unit and get out of Fresh Start as soon as I could. Plus I had Mrs Minsk's mantra about 'eating a live frog in the morning', which is her little way of saying 'do something unpleasant you don't want to do straight away, because once it is over, the rest of the day isn't so bad'. It took me years to work out what this meant. For years I thought Mrs Minsk walked Kitten and me to school and then came home and had a plate of nice live frogs.

Clarion gave us shovels and trowels and told us to begin moving methodically through the mud, discarding rubbish and bagging any interesting objects for the archeology team. I thought the archeology line must be a joke. All I could see was mangled carrier bags, discarded boots and and broken jam jars. Nothing to bother the *Antiques Roadshow* with.

I started work and my mind began to drift. The noise of Striker and Vixen bickering quietly about how they'd even ended up on Fresh Start, and Clarion lecturing on 'life choices', and Blitzen moaning, quickly became background buzz as I contemplated stuff like Hampstead Lycée and the moors in *Wuthering Heights* and who Dragon's real mother was and the bleak findings of Flash's family tree project and Daddy and those ruddy Zambian emeralds that are driving me slightly nuts.

After a few hours, lunchtime was announced and we all had to go and have a good wash. Lunch took the shape of a horrible pre-made sandwich trapped in a bizarre plastic triangle that no one on Fresh Start even knew how open. The choice was 'cheese' or 'ham'. I chose 'cheese' because it was the safer option. I've no idea what sort of ham was in the 'ham' one, but it was see-through and sweaty and seemed to come in squares. I've never seen a square pig. Not even on *Battlestar Galactica.*

'Is this really lunch?' said a boy called Farquar.

We all thought it was a joke and Clarion would soon bring out a nice buffet or at least a vegan option, but, alas the sandwich was lunch.

I managed a few bites and went straight back to work, but I was thinking about Knute's latest protest, for which he was chained to a Virgin Airways 747 at Heathrow's Terminal Five, and I also thought very hard about my sculpture class and how the fact is I'll NEVER finish that

Roman Centurion, NEVER. The truth is, just after the willy fell off I thought I'd be clever and give him a sex change by making the hole where the willy was into a ladygarden, but after a lot more chipping the whole thing just looked rather obscene. But throughout all my thinking on various topics, ranging from the Hubble telescope to my favourite type of sushi to who I'd play in the musical *Mamma Mia* if I was forced at gunpoint to choose a role, one thing never crossed my mind. Kwame.

This pricked my conscience somewhat. I sneaked my iPhone from my boilersuit pocket – they were strictly prohibited – and bashed out a quick message. It said: DAY 1 OK. CLEANING UP RIVER. SPEAK SOON POPZ X

I re-checked the message. Nothing too lovey-dovey. But then I didn't feel lovey-dovey as I was covered in mud. And it's not like Kwame is a flaming ball of passion right now. Last night on the phone all he wanted to talk about was whether I'd revised all the periodic table symbols yet. My text sort of summed up how I felt about that. I sent it and waited for a beep as he always hits me straight back. Nothing happened. TWENTY MINUTES PASSED and then a text arrived, which read: GOOD STUFF. MAILED BO THIS MORNING. SAYS COURSEWORK YOU DID IS MUCH BETTER. U R BACK ON COURSE! KWAM

I stared at the text. No kisses. None. I'd put one, at least. He'd put NONE. And at least my text came under the label of news/gossip. All Kwame wanted to tell me was about was my coursework. But worse than that, worse than ANYTHING, Kwame had called my headmistress – Mrs Boudecia Prendergast – 'Bo'. Bo!!! He was on chummy first name terms with Mrs Prendergast! Somehow, he'd got her private home email and was discussing me with her behind my back.

My innards began to simmer as I pulled rocks and sticks from the mud and threw them into the skip. I knew I was reading stuff into this text that maybe wasn't there but it was difficult not to. Why was Kwame sucking up to my mother and Mrs Prendergast so much? Did he care about me or did he care about getting his tutoring job done successfully as he wanted his cash? Did he even love me any more? Why would there be a twenty-minute turnaround on my text if he loved me? And did I love him? Um, yes, I was pretty sure I did. Almost sure. Ninety-eight per cent positive.

I was fuming and inwardly chuntering so much that I didn't notice the latest goings-on in Fresh camp. A minor rumpus was happening. A new yellow boilersuit had joined our group. A boy with two bodyguards. This had Blitzen's back up already as she clearly thought she'd be the richest person by far on today's course and no one was at more risk than her of being kidnapped by Al Qaeda. But now, someone had turned up with their own security team.

The boy kept his back to us, found a shovel and a patch of mud to work on; meanwhile his two guards stood nearby on the bank, talking on mobile phones.

Their black shiny shoes and pristine, pressed black trousers were getting terribly dirty in the mud. Then one of them spotted something further along the bank he didn't like and signalled to the other that it needed dealing with. 'No photographs!' he yelled at a third figure standing behind a bush.

The new boy in the yellow suit heard the fuss and shrunk slightly in shame, keeping his back turned.

The third man, who was obviously a member of the paparazzi, judging from his weasely face and aggressive tone of voice, shouted, 'I can take photos of whatever I like, this is a public place. I've got rights!'

The security man glared at him hard, left a chilling pause and said, 'You trot back to your editor and ask him to check with Her Majesty what she thinks of your rights. You know the rules. No photos. Don't make your life hard.'

He said this in such a non-nonsense way that the pap immediately put his camera down and slunk off. This was remarkable. Paps never do that. Everyone stared in awe at the burly security man, and then at the new boy he was working for.

'Oh my God, I know who he is,' hissed Striker, letting out a little gleeful shriek. 'It's Prince Frankie. Poppet? It's Frankie Walcott.'

'No way,' I whispered back.

'It jolly well is,' said Vixen.

All three of us stared. Frankie carried on working,

ignoring everyone. I checked out my fellow cog in the British Royal Family, although he's a much higher, faster, more important cog. I'm the cog at the bottom no one cares about, Frankie is properly royal. He's an HRH. His Royal Highness. Although *Heat* says it stands for Hellishly Royal Hottie, because Frankie has grown rather beautiful over recent years. He's not podgy at all now, in fact his whole face just hangs off a pair of incredible cheekbones, framed by rather a lot of eyebrows, which I'd love to get my tweezers to, just for a quick tidy-up, even if it would spoil that part-prince/part-caveman vibe he's got going on.

'Oh my God,' said Vixen, 'the Palace has finally gone mad.'

'You know him, don't you?' said Striker.

'I did years ago,' I said. 'We don't really see that side of the relations now.'

I was certain Frankie wouldn't remember me from when we were tiny so I got back on with work and made myself invisible. From this vantage point, I could enjoy the spellbinding sight of watching Blitzen Trapper turn every trick in the book to grab Frankie's attention. She tried bumping into him accidentally on purpose, then trying to render him catatonic with her insipid chat, but he wasn't in the mood for socializing. She tried helping him with his work, having suddenly and mysteriously overcome her mud phobia, but it was clear Frankie wanted to work alone. At one point Blitzen disappeared from sight into the back of a transit van, returning with the legs on her yellow boilersuit trousers rolled up into capri pants and a makeshift belt made from something she found on the skip, tied to accentuate her curves. Well Clarion lost patience then, for the first time that day. He pulled her to the side and explained that the whole point of the boilersuit uniform was to make us feel anonymous and unglamorous, not individual and full of ego. Clarion told Blitzen to roll the trouser legs down and take the belt off, which was a shame, I thought, as I was relishing her looking so completely daft. Blitzen, however, wasn't deterred by this. It was clear to me that Blitzen had already mentally dumped whoever that boyfriend was with the two broken legs and was imagining her face being printed on the side of the HRH Blitzen Trapper and Francis Walcott commemorative Royal Wedding mugs. Frankie Walcott was Blitzen Trapper's now, even if he didn't know anything about it.

Vixen watched Blitzen fussing about Frankie, who seemed a little cross about it.

'Why can't she give him some space?' Vixen said, in uncharacteristically irate tones.

Today was a very long day indeed. I've never been so glad to see six o'clock. I was even happy to see Voychek. He didn't know how to handle this. He looked quite embarassed when I jumped into the car and asked him how his day had been.

' 'S fine,' he said. 'Quiet day today. Y'know I nearly miss driving you round. You make me laugh. Always horrible to Voychek.'

I laughed when he said that. He did too. Voychek and I shared a laugh. What the heck is going on?

I got a gold star on my Fresh Start report today for my hard work on the Lea Valley canal path. OK, in fairness, a gold star is the type of lame thing you give a two-year-old to reward it for pooing in its potty and not over the side, but at least it made my mother like me.

'Did you enjoy it today?' my mother said when I got home and was raiding the fridge for sustenance.

'Of course I didn't,' I said, dramatically. 'You've put me in hell. I'll never forgive you for this as long as I live.'

'Oh dear,' she said.

'I'm going to put you in a home as soon as you're fifty and never visit you,' I said, eating a double-chocolate fudge cookie.

'Oh good,' smiled Mummy, looking at her Blackberry, unphased by my dramaticism. 'But did it give you time to think about life? That's the point, y'know. You're meant to get distance from your daily life and have time to find yourself.'

'Hmmphh,' I harumphed. Then I gave my dishes to Mrs Minsk and went to my bedroom and lay thinking about what Prince Francis Walcott's bum looked like in a pair of yellow overalls. Fresh Start really is making me think. It's making me more confused than ever.

FRIDAY 26TH FEBRUARY

Today was definitely what Dr Sarzberg the family therapist would probably term 'a wake up call'. I'm lying in my bedroom right now in the bay window on the chaise-longue, that I usually use to dump clothes, surrounded by all the silly possessions I take for granted, all my shoes, hair clips, knickers, socks, books, eyelash curlers etc. and I'm thinking: Oh my Lord, how would I cope if I owned nothing? Not one little thing. If I just owned the skin I'm standing up in.

I've never thought of this before. I've always had stuff, tons of stuff. My earliest ever memories are of Kitten and I running about in an enormous nursery full to the brim with toys and games and an indoors climbing-frame and ball pond. We've always had walk-in wardrobes full of clothes too. I'm always fascinated when I see people's homes on TV and they just have one tiny little wardrobe stuffed full of everything. How do they ever get dressed? But if someone said, 'Poppet, there's a gang coming to kill everyone in Hampstead and all of the Montague-Jones family because they're sick of you poshos and your snooty ways and they're armed with axes and they're going to chop you, so you've just got to run NOW and take nothing if you want to save your own life,' well if that happened, where would I go? How would I manage when I got there if I didn't even have even a toouthbrush or a change of knickers?

I didn't realize that was what being an asylum-seeker is. I didn't realize you literally washed up in another country, running for your life, with nothing, only the clothes you were wearing the day you ran off. No passport, no money, no suitcase, just you.

And people are really vile about asylum-seekers too. Like Blitzen Trapper was today when we were waiting in the minibus outside Fresh Start HQ in Belsize Park.

'Oh God, please, like we should feel sorry for asylum-seekers,' she said. 'Give me a break. The country is flooded with them.'

Clarion coughed disapprovingly when Blitzen said that, but Blitzen carried on. 'My daddy says Great Britain is the laughing stock of the world,' she said. 'We just let anyone in with a hard-luck story then give them money. He says they should be sent home to where they came from. They're just scroungers!'

Just at that moment the minibus fell silent as Prince Frankie boarded with his two security guards. I felt bad for Frankie. I wished everyone in the group would treat him a bit more normally. People act incredibly odd around royalty, really self-conscious or sycophantic – even the Fresh Start kids and they're all due to inherit billions anyway – without the added hassle of being in line to the throne. Seeing him again up close has reminded me how being royal is rather a pain in the neck. I'm so glad I'm eighty-seventh and no lower. I'd rather not be royal at all but I'm not allowed to say that out loud as people get all jealous and cross.

'Frankie, here's a seat!' said Blitzen, tapping the last remaining empty space on the bus, which was beside her. The seat was vacant as everyone else in the group had sussed by now that she's a horrid piece of work. Just like I did in Year Seven when she told everyone she'd seen my toes up close in the school shower and they were webbed. I spent the first eight weeks at Hampstead Lycée with girls quacking at me in the corridors and calling me Donaldina Duck. I will never forgive Blitzen for that, ever. Even if I pretend I've forgotten.

I was sitting on the middle seat on the back row, as Frankie made his way up the minibus to the vacant seat. He was staring straight at me, or through me. Frankie sat down, then turned his body round to take a second look at me.

'Hello,' I said, in a small voice.

'Hello,' he said, quickly turning away. Then suddenly he swung his entire body round, looked me right in the eye with a huge grin lighting up his face, and said, 'Poppet Montague-Jones?'

'Hello, Frankie!' I said.

'Oh my goodness!' he said. 'I've not seen you for, like, ages. You're, erm, much, erm different! How are you?'

'Great,' I said. Fantastic!

'How's Kitten?' he said.

'Oh she's good. She's straight-edge now, it's sort of funny,' I told him.

'Really?' he said. 'I saw Knute in the paper last week! He tried to wrestle that guy in Thailand. That politician.'

'Oh yeah,' I giggled. 'Knute's saving the world. It's a dangerous job.'

Striker and Vixen were staring right at Frankie all the time I was saying this – I knew they were dying to be introduced.

'Frankie, this is Striker Earhart and Vixen Diaz-Brocklehurst, they're my friends from Lycée.'

'Hello, Frankie,' said Vixen, who had broken into a light sweat. Vixen is never ever like this. She's usually utterly unflappable.

'Hey,' smiled Striker, chewing her gum, then getting her iPhone out of her pocket to check her texts as if to say, *Oh, so you're Royal? Puh-lease. You'll need to try a lot harder than that to impress me.*

'Delighted to meet you both,' he said.

Frankie's voice is a lot posher than mine. I get told off all the time by Mummy for talking 'like a chav' and slipping a very occasional 'innit' into a sentence. Frankie sounds more like my granny's close friend Sir Peregrine Folstoy-Muir who has to have subtitles underneath his face whenever he talks on television about architecture as nobody aside from his butler can actually understand him.

'So you're well, then?' Frankie said. 'I've not talked to you since . . .'

I wanted to say, 'Since Kitten tied your annoying

sister's plaits to a door in the 1990s then slammed it shut and almost scalped her?' but I knew this wasn't the cheeriest memory to evoke.

'Oh, I'm fine,' I said. 'I mean I'm here, so maybe some people don't think I'm doing so brilliantly.'

'Well yes, obviously,' grinned Frankie. (I'd forgotten how green his eyes were.) 'What happened?'

'Mmm well,' I began, conscious that twenty people including Clarion were intently listening.

'I'll ask you later,' he said, and he winked.

'Yes, do,' I said. Then he turned to look straight ahead again.

Now I'm not a big fan of winking, but this was a good wink. It wasn't a pervy wink or a cheesy wink, it was sort of a lovely cheeky wink. A sexy wink, if that thing exists. Or maybe I imagined that. Or maybe everything Frankie does is slightly sexy. Or maybe I'm starting to go mental.

'Dude, he's like your cousin or something. Gross,' whispered Striker, chewing gum and looking at her iPhone.

'He's NOT my ruddy cousin,' I whispered. 'He's very very *very* distantly related. Not even related at all really. We're just both part of the same ancestral line. That's different. Anway, I only said hello to him.'

'Oof, touchy. I'm only winding you up,' Striker said. 'I don't think you want to jump him or anything.'

'GOOD because I don't,' I said. 'I'm with Kwame. I don't want to jump him.'

'Hang on,' said Striker, putting her phone down. 'I do think that now. Definitely. Sensitive, much?'

'Pah,' I said, pretending to listen intently to Clarion as he began telling us all about our destination. Vixen was laughing loudly now and Striker was trying to tickle me to pay her some attention.

Clarion was talking about the asylum-seekers' refuge we were visiting in Wood Green – well this just got Blitzen chuntering again about how these people managed to have their own house when they didn't pay tax, and this was why we needed to seal up Britain's borders and send people back off on boats to where they came from, and stop giving people handouts because that's why there was so many of them coming, and someone had told her that was why people were catching Tuberculosis, she'd read this in her cleaner's copy of the *Daily Mail*.

Clarion listened to this for a while and then he said, 'Blitzen, aren't your family Russian?'

'My daddy is American and my mummy is Russian,' Blitzen said. 'But Mummy's family have lived in America for years. Like since the 1920s. They're American now.'

'Really,' he said. 'So how did they all end up in America?'

Blitzen thought for a second.

'I don't know. They just went there,' she said. 'They all moved there in the 1930s.'

'They just fancied a change?' said Clarion.

Blitzen tutted. 'I don't know,' she said. 'They're

Jewish. They wanted to be near other Jewish people. They left Noyabrsk and went to East Side, New York. But then everyone wants to leave Noyabrsk. It's hideous. I went with Mummy last year. They don't even have wi-fi. It's just lots of poor people with bad skin drinking potato-liqueur and dying in shop doorways.'

Clarion didn't say anything. A couple of people laughed. The annoying thing about Blitzen is, despite being a bitch, she's got a nifty way with words. People don't tend to challenge her, only this time Clarion was.

'So they left Noyabrsk through choice?' Clarion said.

Blitzen tutted loudly as if his questions were annoying her. 'Well, it was something to do with politics too,' she said. 'I think one of my great-grandmother's friends was shot dead outside a synagogue.'

'I see,' he said.

We drove along in silence.

Blitzen sat looking at her iPhone. I wondered when the penny was going to drop for her, like it had for all of us. Had she realized that her family were basically asylum-seekers at one point too. Does the penny ever drop for people like Blitzen? Or are they born with some sort of reality-proof Vulcanized rubber coating. Maybe Blitzen is actually the lucky one. I can't work out whether starting to think about the world had made me happier or sadder. Blitzen is what grown-ups mean by 'blissfully ignorant', isn't she?

Just then, Boyd, a quiet Jewish boy who up to

now hadn't really spoken piped up. 'Blitzen, your grandparents were most probably asylum-seekers.' Well you could have heard a gnat fart at this point, the minibus went so silent. 'Two million Jews had to get out of Russia at the turn of the nineteenth century as they were being persecuted; they were forbidden to work or go to synagogues, and being starved to death and having their money stolen by the banks. If America hadn't let your family have asylum there, you'd not be here. You wouldn't exist.'

There was a silence. Then Farquar said, 'Oh my God, Blitzy, you're an asylum-seeker! Where should we send you back to?'

Well everyone laughed then, mainly due to the break in the hideous tension.

'Oh God, whatever,' said Blitzen, shaking her head as if to say, *Why is everyone picking on me?*

The minibus pulled up outside an enormous, ramshackle house, which at one point had been a vicarage, but was now an asylum-seekers' refuge. I was feeling rather nervous by now. After everything Clarion had said and Boyd's bits about being shot at and starved to death, I was scared to leave the nice, warm minibus. I was imagining a whole house of insane, wounded, scary people rocking and mooing and trying to steal my wallet.

In reality, Smallwood Mansions was just a big, rather threadbare five-storey house with a leaking roof, with a peculiar smell of feet and pickled beetroot and around eighty-five rather depressed people from Rwanda, Kurdistan, Afghanistan and Iraq, including lots of little children, looking a bit lost and watching daytime telly.

I wanted to leave the minute I arrived. I can't imagine what being there for a whole year would do to your mind.

A woman called Shyaka from Rwanda who helps run the place explained to us that she came here after the war in her country that ended in genocide. I didn't know what genocide was but I do now and it's vile. In fact I don't want to think about it again ever. Shyaka said that if you flee to Britain as an asylum-seeker then you're running for your life, so you don't bring any belongings or paperwork to prove who you are. So you can't really do anything, get a bank account or apply for a job or anything. And you're not really legally meant to be here, so the government won't let you work anywhere to support yourself. So you're kind of stuck in the middle of being alive and safe, but not being a real person who anyone cares about. You could just be here at Smallwood Mansions, which I was deciding now smelled of old underpants gone fusty on a radiator mixed with the spray Mrs Minsk uses to kill bluebottles in summer, for ever.

After the little talk, which even managed to render Blitzen Trapper silent and vaguely moved, so it must have been powerful, Clarion revealed a rota and put us all to work. Striker and Farquar were to help people who didn't speak English to fill in forms, Vixen and two girls called Betty and Jonquella were sorting bags of donated second-hand books and toys and giving them a scrub. Some of the boys were given screwdrivers and told to help some of the Iraqi men put IKEA cots together for a lot of new babies who had just arrived. My job was in the attic laundry, ironing sheets and clothes and putting together basic starter packs for new arrivals. Bars of soap, toothbrushes, fresh pants, a pair of socks, just basic stuff to make people feel more like humans again. It felt really good to be able to help people.

'Poppet, you'll be working with Boyd and Frankie,' Clarion said as we all stood in the hallway of the house. Blitzen stared at me furiously. I'm sure she'd much prefer being up in the attic with Frankie and not stuck behind an enormous pile of unpeeled carrots in the kitchen, helping with tonight's dinner. Blitzen began mumbling something to Clarion, who said, 'But Blitzen, you've got to remember that this could be some people's first hot meal for weeks.'

'God, what is up with these retards?' sneered Blitzen. 'There's a Wagamama on every corner in London. The Ramen noodles are priced very reasonably, eleven pounds a bowl. What are they, ruddy helpless?'

I couldn't help but laugh at that. I climbed the stairs up into the loft, immediately realizing I'd got the cushiest deal as it was warm and cosy up there and the air smelled of lovely sweet fabric conditioner. Frankie followed me though the door with Boyd behind him, both carrying armfuls of freshly-laundered bed sheets.

'Go on then, Poppet,' Frankie said. 'What are you in Fresh Start for?'

'Oh heck,' I said, blushing a little. 'It's totally embarrassing. I'm not really here for anything.' The two boys groaned and laughed at that.

'You must be here for something, Poppet,' Frankie laughed. 'We're all here for something. I messed up, I admit it. Boyd is here for flying to Vegas and losing five hundred thousand pounds playing Roulette.'

'It was three hundred and eighty-five thousand pounds actually,' Boyd said. 'I, erm, well, I spent the other one hundred and fifteen thousand pounds on suites for me and my friends at the Bellagio hotel.'

'Wow,' I said. That was actually, weirdly impressive.

'See, we're all in here for something,' said Frankie. 'So, do you want to confess?'

'No, but you don't understand,' I said. 'I'm in here for NOTHING. OK, I started seeing a boy from the Cottingham Estate in Kilburn. And my parents were, like, freaking out as he was from a bad estate.'

'OK,' said Frankie. Boyd had stopped what he was doing now, waiting for the juicy part of my story to begin.

'And my grades were getting really low at Hampstead Lycée, I mean, like I was getting Ds in English.'

'Right,' said Boyd. 'D's not that bad. I mean, it's not good, but it's not terrible.'

'Yes, but then my friend, Striker,' I said, 'y'know the girl with the peroxide cropped hair and the, well, y'knows . . .'

I mimed her plentiful bust and sexy expression.

'Yes,' they both said, without pausing. Everyone knows who Striker is. She's the girl who needs no re-introducing.

'Well, Striker was caught shoplifting in Bodwin's Boutique on the CCTV, and she stayed out all night with her ex-boyfriend, Bizzle, who had an electronic tag on his ankle as he'd been caught dealing cocaine.'

'Ooof, naughty,' said Frankie. Boyd drew closer, waiting for the big finish.

'And that's it,' I said.

'That's it?' said Boyd. 'What did you do?'

'I told you,' I said.

'You got a D grade in an essay and your friend got into some trouble?' he laughed. 'Why the hell are you here?'

'I KNOW,' I said. 'That's what I say!'

'Oh my Lord, you were STITCHED UP,' said Frankie. The boys were both really laughing at me now. It was the first genuine, hysterical belly-laugh I'd heard since the course started.

'It's not funny,' I said, 'they've threatened to disinherit me. I've got this horrible driver who's this Polish ex-military . . . Hey guys, listen.' I tried to finish the sentence but they were laughing too much to listen.

I began to giggle then. I realized that if this wasn't my life I'd find it really rib-tickling.

'OK, OK, OK!' I said. 'Come on then, Frankie. Tell me what you did.'

Frankie stopped laughing and looked vaguely sheepish.

'Oh come on, you must know,' he said. 'I thought everyone knew.'

'No, I don't,' I said. I'd done a bit of investigating on the night after Frankie first joined us on the canal path, but there was nothing on any of the gossip websites or news sites.

'Right,' sighed Frankie. 'I suppose that press injunction my mother took out has worked, then, as none of the newspapers have reported it.'

'Reported what?' Boyd and I chorused.

'Oh God, it's shameful really. Look I'm not proud of this. It's not cool and I won't be doing it again. I've been an idiot.'

'OK,' we agreed impatiently. Holy hell, this was sounding good already.

'So I went to Farenheit Club last week with Margot and Jocelyn,' he said. 'Now I'm not supposed to go to Farenheit and the palace has told my security guards not to let me go there as it's bad for the Royal Family's reputation and blah blah blah, right? So the security guards told Farenheit they should stop letting me in anyway as I'm under eighteen and they'd lose their drinks licence. But I got in anyway.'

'How?' I said.

'Well, what the palace keep forgetting is that since Margot turned twenty-one, she actually inherited the plot of land that Farenheit Club is on. It's her lease on the name to the owner. And the owner, Paolo, is trying to get planning permission to extend the club and build a roof terrace now and Margot has to sign that off, so if Margot wants me to come to the club it's her that has to say yes.'

'So you can always get in, no matter what?' I said.

'Well no, not now,' he winced. 'I've messed up so badly. Seriously. See, when I went out last week I was in a really terrible mood. I was totally stressed out by this meeting my father made me have with our accountant about my assets and inheritance and where I want to start channelling it.'

This sounded familiar. I've started picking up my phone to Mr Chenowitz when he rings me to moan about fiscal proceedures on transporting back from Hong Kong the rare Ming vases that Great-aunt Persephone left me and saying, 'Can I call you back, Mr Chenowitz, I'm having a big poo?' And this is when I'm not even having a big poo. Or even sitting on the loo at all. It's just the most shocking thing I can think of to stop him nagging me. I wanted to tell Frankie the 'big poo' bit but I wasn't sure if it was appropriate so instead I said, 'It stresses me out too, I hate thinking about it.'

'Well my father crowbarred his way into the meeting,' he said, 'and started nagging me about having no direction in my life, saying I should have started a company by now because he'd had three companies by the time he was eighteen. And I said, "Yeah, Dad but they all failed and one of them was supplying organic marmalade to Japan and you only sold three jars and the company cost you thirty thousand pounds to set up," and he got really angry then. He said I was becoming an unsightly stain on the face of the Royal Family and he'd had enough of me.'

Frankie sounded rather het up just thinking about it. I don't think parents actually think we're listening and taking it in when they say things like, 'You're an embarassment to the family!' but of course we are. Of course it hurts us. We just pretend it doesn't because then they'd know they've won.

'So I stormed out of the house and went to Farenheit with my sisters and I was knocking back shots of that liqueur called Absinthe. Do you know, the green one that makes you hallucinate.'

'I don't drink,' said Boyd, shaking his head.

'Neither do I, now,' said Frankie, ruefully. 'Well, the last thing I remember is ordering two bottles of Absinthe for all the people in the booth I was sitting in. And apparently the waiter tried to stop me, but I was being a complete arse-head and saying things like, " 'I'm the ruddy future King of England, I'll have you all executed at dawn, you ruddy pleb!" '

'You didn't say that, really?' I said, cringing.

'Yes, I did, but I was joking! Seriously, Poppet, I absolutely was. I thought I was a comedy genius. I felt like a solo stand-up artist playing the 02 arena and everyone was hanging on my every hilarious word.'

'So did he have you thrown you out?' I said.

'No, he bought me the Absinthe,' said Frankie. 'And I started drinking it, and from that moment on it's all blank, until my security guards found me at five a.m., lying asleep in a pile of bin bags around the back of the club.'

'Oh God,' I said. Boyd was laughing.

'And a dog had taken a wazz all over my jeans and shoes,' he said.

'And the paparazzi had taken photos and already emailed them to Buckingham Palace press office and to the editor of *The Sun*.'

'Oh noooooo,' I said.

'And MI5 thought I'd been kidnapped by Al Qaeda so they'd already deployed security to search for me. They had helicopters out and everything. And my father is billing me for the helicopters.'

'Fail. Majestic fail,' said Boyd.

'No, it's worse than that,' he said. 'Well I was in a really dodgy state and they thought I'd done myself serious damage. I was rushed to A & E under a secret name. And they pumped my stomach, and in the meantime my mother was taking out a court injunction against the newspapers to stop them printing pictures of me covered in dog wee and vomit.'

'Oh Lordy,' I said, really rather shocked.

'I know. Frankie picked up an enormous white sheet

and tried to fold it, but got mixed up as it was clearly the first time he'd ever done this by himself before. Eventually he put the sheet down in a crumpled ball and just stared sadly at it. 'Well, I made a right mess of that,' he said.

'Never mind,' I told him. 'I suppose some of the people who arrive here today will have spent the last two days clinging to the undercarriage of a Eurostar train, so anything else will be an improvement.'

'Yes,' said Frankie, who seemed quite sad now. I don't think he was very proud of the ambulance/Absinthe/dog wee/court injunction story.

'So what are you thinking now?' I said, walking across to him and rubbing his arm. I wanted to give him a little hug but it might have been weird.

'Oh I just want to sort all this stuff out,' he said, 'I want to be different. I want to feel like I'm doing some good. Not just being some mega-rich dung-head who annoys everyone all the time. I feel like giving all my money and my title away.'

'Same here,' I said, 'I want to feel like I'm the one in the family history book on the force of good not evil. Do you know what I mean?'

'Are your family in *Star Wars*?' said Boyd.

We all cracked up then.

'You know what I mean,' I said.

'Yes,' said Frankie, 'I completely know.'

And then we looked at each other. It was only a little

look that lasted maybe a millionth more than a normal look would, but it made me feel very peculiar indeed.

The atmosphere on the minibus home tonight was rather subdued. Vixen and the girls who'd been working with the tiny kids today seemed the most downbeat. Vixen had been doing a jigsaw and playing Hide and Seek with a little girl called Aziza who was especially timid as she'd seen some horrible violent things happen to her dad, before the family ran away. Apparently, as Vixen was leaving, she'd said to Clarion, 'Well at least she's safe now.' Clarion replied, 'Well actually, the government don't believe she's unsafe in Somalia so she's probably being sent back.'

Well that was game over for Vixen. I know Vixen chose to be on Fresh Start as she wanted to 'awaken her perception' and 'broaden her cerebral horizons' but I think by tonight her mind had been awoken and broadened quite enough. I'm sure she's lying in a darkened room right now with whale music playing and her lavender sticks burning.

When Vixen told Striker Aziza's story on the minibus today, a peculiar thing happened. Striker took her iPhone out of her bag and called her father. I pretended not to listen as she left a message saying she was sorry she'd not returned his last twenty or so calls, but she was calling him now and maybe they could like, erm, chat. Striker hung up the phone and looked like she regretted it immediately but it was done and that was that. I knew Striker knew that I heard, but I didn't ask her to explain. She knows I'm here for her when she wants to talk.

Another surprise was Blitzen. I fully expected her to jump back on the bus making offensive statements about how the place had given her fleas and she needed to lie in a bath of bleach, or at least mock the funny clothes all the asylum-seekers were wearing as everyone just has to wear whatever they're given, so they're not exactly fashionable. But she didn't say anything horrid at all.

I did have a little giggle however as we were reaching Hampstead as Blitzen's phone rang and I heard her saying. 'Oh hi, Amelia, how's it going? Oh good good. Oh I'm so jealous. I love Dries Van Noten. Wow, their dresses are beautiful. He bought you two? I was on the front row for their last show. I was sitting with Heidi Klum. She has cellulite on her knees, did I ever say? How's it going here?' (Pause here while Blitzen wondered whether to lie or not to save face.) 'It's dreadful actually. Dreadful. I can't quite tell you how so. I can't get my head round it. It's just awful. These people are in . . . well they're in hell. Yes, I know they're scroungers. But they have to scrounge. They're totally desperate, Amelia. I would scrounge. You either scrounge or you'd die. Look, stop it, you've not seen them and I have. Shut up, Amelia. Anyway, listen, exciting news.' Blitzen double-checked to see if Frankie, who'd been dozing since we left the hostel, was still in the land of nod. 'Amelia, seriously, I'm so IN. He's seriously taking the bait. Yes. Totally. How? I just know. I can tell. He's always looking at me with this really amazed expression when I speak. Saying that, you should see the state of the other girls so it's not hard to shine. But no, we've had a few chats and I've got him in the zone. Seriously spam-armed women in Essex will be buying royal tea-towels with my face on by the end of the year. Her Royal Highness Princess Blitzen.' Well Blitzen cracked up laughing then.

I felt like running down the minibus and shaking Frankie furiously yelling, 'Wake up dumbo! Can't you see this hideous, cruel-hearted girl is trying to trap you! Save yourself damnit!' But that would have looked a bit odd, bearing in mind it's none of my business who either of them go out with.

And why do I care what happens to Frankie Walcott? I'm with Kwame. And he's allowed around to my house now whenever he wants. He was there tonight waiting for me when I got home as he was leaving some Physics GCSE past papers. Kwame, my mother, Kitten and Flash were sitting in the kitchen at the table drinking tea and eating cake.

'Hey, Poppet,' he said, when I appeared in the kitchen.

'Hey you,' I said, picking up the past papers and snorting hot air down both nostrils.

'Kwame and I have made a deal,' Mummy said, smiling.

'We've decided that if you get through that paper this evening with a C grade or higher, then Kwame can take you out for a pizza. On your own. No Voychek.'

I stared at them, sitting there smiling back at me. You're one of them now, Kwame, I thought. You've switched sides and now you're just one of them. The boring people who make the rules. You even dress a bit like them and speak the same language they do. But I stopped myself saying it as I knew I'd just sound hysterical.

'Can we not just go for the pizza anyway?' I said. 'I'm starving.

'Do a paper first, Poppet,' said Kwame. 'Then we'll go. That's the deal I made with your mum. It's only forty-five minutes. Why don't you go upstairs and do it now. I'll wait here for you.'

'Wow, Poppet,' said Kitten fake-dreamily, sipping her herbal tea, 'that's so romantic. That's like movie-love.'

'Shut up, Kitten,' I snapped, then walked huffily up here and got into bed.

I am NOT doing a Physics GCSE past paper. NO WAY. I've just got home. I'm tired and my head is addled. If those dur-brains think I'm up here doing it, then more fool them. I'm going to leave it a little while longer then write something unrepeatable on it and give it back. Let's see what grade Kwame Kobina wants to give me for that.

SUNDAY 28TH FEBRUARY

5 P.M.

Over the last few hours, lying here brooding in my bedroom, once more cast out of the Montague-Jones family, branded as a dangerous and nefarious influence, I've been mulling over the thought; Am I really such a bad person? and Could I have tried any harder to stop the collapse of my reputation? and Poppet Zanzibar Montague-Jones, how did things go so very, very wrong?

Mummy is exceptionally irate with me right now. She's in that white-heat stage of lividness where she can't actually speak. Incandescent. Apopleptic. APOCALYPTIC even. I'd far rather she was in my room, ranting and whirling both arms like a psychotic nutbag, threatening to send me to an American-Mormon boarding school in Dubai. Or threatening, like she did last week during the Donna Karan coat incident, to hire me a full-time nanny to follow me round, just like Olivia Brightwell's nanny, Mrs Tiggy. Mummy was very expressive and noisy then. Not serene at all.

'Right!' she yelled. 'That's it, you are clearly INCAPABLE of acting like a normal, decent human being. I'm hiring someone to ASSIST YOU!'

Mummy was in the middle of getting ready for an important pitch to a potential client and the more she hyperventilated, the more she missed her mouth with her lipstick.

'I'm hiring you someone in a navy-blue pinafore,' she screamed. 'Twenty-four-hour supervision! Someone who'll put you to bed at nine p.m., with your jimjams warmed by the fire and a teacup of milk with honey.'

'You wouldn't dare!' I shouted.

'Try me!' she shouted back, lipstick all over her teeth. She looked a lot like a waxwork dummy from the London Dungeons.

'I AM trying you!' I shouted.

'Well I'm just going to research some nanny websites now, on my way to my meeting,' shouted my mother, waving her Blackberry. 'Hold tight: you'll have a nanny by tomorrow morning.'

At this point my father wandered into the room, stared forlornly at the pair of us, then wandered out again. Daddy left to go on emergency business in his Lagos office shortly afterwards. This was most curious as I checked on the internet and his company don't have a Lagos office.

Mother was flipping out as I'd borrowed her black belted Donna Karan mac to take Macbeth out for a wee in. What a disaster. I'd only had the ruddy coat on ten minutes when I sat on a big blob of half-chewed Hubba Bubba on a park bench in Octavia Square. Well, I panicked then as I knew Mummy loved this coat and I ran home, half-remembering something I read in a magazine about freezing chewing gum in your kitchen freezer, then chipping it off. Only, the gum didn't chip off. It TORE off, leaving a big hole. Well I really panicked then and stuffed the coat under my bed to hide it, but while I was out jogging with Kitten the bloody dog smelled the half-eaten Mars bar I'd left in the coat pocket then dragged the ripped, soggy jacket into the hallway.

Macbeth really is the worst dog ever. She's an idiot. She's the direct opposite of dogs you see on the news who are taken into earthquake zones and help people.

When Mummy found the remnants of her new spring/summer chocolate-smeared ripped designer purchase she had a severe sense-of-humour by-pass and began screaming lots of rude things.

But that's the crucial difference between then and the state of play now. Today the house is in absolute SILENCE. My mother is absolutely SHOCKED AND OUTRAGED. I think she really believed Fresh Start was one place I couldn't get up to mischief. Oh how wrong she was. But if she ruddy spoke to me about what she's read in the papers she'd know it is mostly untrue.

This is what happened. The papers should print this.

At about seven p.m. last night, Voychek drove Vixen, Striker and I to a homeless shelter called Elms Place Facility down by the River Thames. The atmosphere in the car was chatty although we were all pretty anxious about what was in store for us. Striker was talking about a homeless guy she'd met outside Starbucks in Hampstead last week and how she'd ended up hearing his life story and buying him a frappuccino with extra caramel syrup, and Voychek was listening intently and even turned Talk London FM off. I was totally expecting Voychek to start grouching on about how homeless people needed to be locked up, thrown in a pit, or made to work breaking rocks in the midday sun in chain gangs, but he took me by surprise.

'Homeless can happen to anyone,' Voychek said, pointing at a man sitting begging beside a cash machine in an Esso garage forecourt. 'It happen very easy if you've not got savings for rainy day. If you get ill and not be able to work for two months and you miss mortgage, bang, you homeless.'

We didn't say anything to that. That could never happen to my family. My family have got money hidden all over the ruddy world. I've got an offshore bank account in my name in Andorra with 2.8 million pounds in it I'm not even meant to know about. I only found out as Mr Chenowitz went to the loo in one of our meetings and I picked up a random piece of paper in my file. Turns out Granny has been shoving extra bits of money she doesn't want to pay tax on into it.

'But if you're homeless,' Vixen said, 'can't you get a home again if you work?'

'Well, most people build life back up,' Voychek said. 'But if you not strong, you end up like that man there.

Filthy, begging for scraps off people.' As our car hit heavy traffic, we watched as crowds of office workers just passed the man by like he was invisible. He kept picking the cup up and waving it, but people walked by, turning their faces away.

'I bet that man had house and wife at one point,' Voychek said. 'Maybe he still got wife somewhere.'

If the homeless guy did still have a wife, she'd need to have a very impaired sense of smell to want him as he was encrusted with ten years of mud, feg and wee, like Oscar the grouch off *Sesame Street*, but less hygienic.

'Loads of these people are totally wacked out on drugs,' Striker said sadly. 'I mean, God, who can blame them. They must just want to get off their faces all the time as it must be so horrid. You're never really safe out here? Are you?' Then she said, 'Hey! Do you remember that time I had the massive argument with my mother in Year Nine and I ran out of the house in the middle of the night and tried to run away from home? Every street I ran down was full of weirdos or drunks. I lasted one whole hour. I was banging on the front door, screaming to get back in.'

'That was awful,' I laughed. 'But really quite funny too.'

Vixen seemed distracted, then she said, 'Do you guys remember when our family had that homeless man sleeping in our summerhouse? About ten years ago. It was during a really bad winter? My daddy didn't even know he was there for two months as the garden is so long. He was this weird hairy man. He'd set up a little bed and he'd been wrapping himself in newspapers and old blankets. And he had some novels and some candles to read with and a tin opener and he'd been living on beans . . .'

'Oh I remember that!' I said.

'Oh my God, yes!' said Striker.

'And then Daddy found out and he was furious with him as he could have set the shed on fire,' said Vixen. 'So he made him go away.'

'Where to?' I said.

'I don't know,' Vixen said. 'He could have gone anywhere I suppose. I'm sure he wouldn't have anywhere specific to go, would he? Actually I don't want to think about it. It's too sad.'

We all sat in silence then. I was remembering how, after the man was made to leave, Vixen and I crept inside when her nanny was distracted and we looked at his books and his old manky duvet, but then Vixen's housekeeper caught us and got all het up about germs and threw all his things in a bin bag and flung them in a wheeliebin. I bet he'd not finished his books. He'll never know what happened. Why was I worrying about this? It was ten years ago.

We pulled up outside the shelter. Voychek looked at us all sternly and told us all to be very careful and that he'd be waiting outside at seven a.m., but if we needed him before, we had to call him and he'd come immediately.

'Poppet, you have my number? Give girls my number,' he told me.

'Yes, Voychek, don't worry,' I said. But I knew Voychek *was* worried and I suppose that this was the point when it hit me that we were actually going to be in a central London shelter meeting desperate drug addicts and the mentally ill. Suddenly all the warning words Clarion had given us the day before came flooding through my head. I was scared.

As we hopped from the car, a black Mercedes drew up on the kerb behind us. Three rather large men in suits jumped out and one of them opened the back door to let HRH Prince Francis Walcott out. I'm sure Frankie would've sneaked into Elms Place Facility unnoticed if it weren't for his bouncers, but now heaps of tourists were staring at his very royal loveliness and floppy hair and magnificent cheekbones, and pulling out cameras and walking towards him with mobile phones, saying, 'Can you record a message for my gran!' I think Frankie's guards cause more havoc than he'd get without them, but apparently Her Majesty the Queen is very scared about all the young A-list royals getting kidnapped. I don't think she's so bothered about what happened to me. Especially after this evening. I think after tonight the thought of me going missing would be a relief and save M15 a hit job.

'Hey Fraaaaaaaankie!' we all chorused, like the most

girlishly girls ever in the history of girldom.

'Poppet!' Frankie said, signing a piece of paper for a little boy 'And . . . um, ladies!'

Ha! Frankie couldn't remember Vixen and Striker's names. I knew this was paining him as he'd hidden it very well and he didn't want them to know. But I knew. The fact that a hot boy had forgotten my friends' names but knew mine was a very unique experience. I've spent the last few years being called 'thingy', and 'her with the metal in her mouth'.

'Come on, we're late!' Frankie said, 'It's ten past seven. Clarion will be vexed in the extreme.'

'I know,' said Striker, 'time is of the essence. These homeless people keep a tight schedule.'

'I dare you to say that to Clarion's face,' laughed Frankie.

'Frankie, don't dare Striker to do anything,' I said, shaking my head furiously.

We wandered into the building, Vixen first, Striker next, then Frankie, and me last, but just as Frankie reached the door, he took a step back and said to me, 'Ladies first,' then lightly cupped my waist and whisked me through. Now, on reflection, this was a crucial moment where I should have said to myself: *Woah there, Popz, get a grip of yourself. LISTEN where your brain seems to be leading you! Let's think about Fresh Start and why you've ended up here? Let's consider your mother's current opinion of you and how you're meant to be progressing and building on this. Let's try and do the RIGHT THING for once in your silly life!* But I couldn't think anything remotely sensible because the small patch of flesh on my waist where Frankie's lovely hand had touched me was communicating via my central nervous system's gnarly mass of receptors and effectors a very strong message to my brain: *HOLY MOTHER OF JESUS, HRH FRANKIE JUST TOUCHED MY WAIST! OMG! OMG OMG OMG! OH HOW MUCH DO I WANT TO GRAB HIM BY THE EARS AND DRAG HIM IN THAT CLOAKROOM AND DO ALL SORTS OF UNSPEAKABLE LUSTFUL THINGS TO HIM THAT CERTAINLY DON'T INVOLVE SITTING AT A KITCHEN TABLE PLODDING SLOWLY THROUGH THE* PHYSICS IN ACTION *GCSE COURSEBOOK! OH GOD, FRANKIE, YOU ARE SUCH A SEXPOT MIOOOOOOOOOOW!'* And my heart wasn't going at a regular bump, bump, bump pace now – it was hammering along at badabadabadab dabdaba pace! And suddenly the air smelled sweet like butter popcorn and the moon was smiling down in its crescent form surrounded by the most jocund and vivacious stars in the galaxy!

OK, I may be exaggerating. Especially about the smell in the air and the celestial formation, but I need to mark it here in my diary that it really was jolly exciting indeed! And, yes, I know I'm going out with Kwame and I know that makes me a duplicitous honest to goodness cow, but Frankie touching my waist was the most exciting thing that had happened to me in the boy department in

MONTHS. Well, ever since the depressing moment Kwame started working as a paid servant to my mother and his good chum, 'Bo'.

And YES, I know it's no excuse for what's occurred, it really isn't. I know I'm the worst human being imaginable. I know I SUCK. I feel like buying a ticket right now and sending myself to that Mormon boarding school in Dubai that doesn't allow iPhones, iPods, iPads, iChat or anything else with an 'i' on the front that lets you live within the twenty-first century. Maybe that's exactly what I need.

So, Vixen, Striker, Frankie, Volka, Boyd, Farquar and myself, (no Blitzen, thank God, as she has 'a twenty-four hour virus') began our shift from ten p.m. to seven a.m.

Elms Place clientele are a diverse but highly raggle-taggle bunch of human beings. They're mostly men but some women, although it's hard to tell the women are women any more until you look very close. Us 'volunteers' were doing things like giving out soup and bread to the homeless people, helping dispense blankets and pillows, giving out shampoo and toothbrushes, helping people who couldn't write fill out forms, or simply chatting to the customers or playing cards with them.

I think chatting to people was one of the most important things I did. Being homeless must be very lonely as people won't look at you, so it felt good to remind someone that they were a real non-invisible human being. I was scared about talking to people at first and spent a few hours hiding in the kitchen stirring soup, but then Striker forced me to sit with her in the canteen area and play some cards. I ended up helping a woman with a broken arm (she'd broken it in a fight) to cut her dinner up, which was only a hot dog but the woman needed it in little bits as she hardly had any teeth (she'd lost them in a fight too). And then I met this man from Belfast in Northern Ireland called Fin. Fin was about forty-five, pretty ancient, but he kept telling me that he'd run off from his mother and father and he couldn't go back. This made him sound a bit mad as he was far too old to live with his mother anyway, but then I started to realize Fin was A LOT mad as he was talking to me and another imaginary person called Stevie inside his brain at the same time.

'Why did you run away?' I said.

'I rubbed some people up the wrong way,' he said, 'didn't we, Stevie? We had to get out of town. So we hopped on the Larne ferry to Stranraer. Then we made our way to Londinium. That was in 1988. Or '89. In the 80s. Yes. Anyway, we're still trying to get ourselves sorted out. Shut up, Stevie! *I* am anyway. He's a nightmare, so he is.'

I don't want to sound negative but Fin didn't look like the 'sorting himself out' was going terribly well. His breath stank of cider and sick, and his skin was filthy and covered in bruises and sores, although I kept noticing he had lovely kind brown eyes, which kept making me think that underneath all the muck and mental health issues maybe Fin was a normal person not much different to my daddy.

'Fin, can you not smooth things out with the people in Belfast?' I said. 'Say you're sorry to them? If the thing you did was a long time ago?'

Fin just shook his head when I said that.

'No, I won't go back. They sorted my friend Donal out, they did. I won't go back. They'll not do me.'

Fin mimed a gun with his fingers and then put it to his kneecap and said, 'Bang.' I felt rather faint when he did that. I think he must have been joking. Why would anyone go around blowing people's kneecaps off? What would that solve? Maybe it was something he imagined, as he was so mad. I'd heard the shelter workers nagging him to take his medication. He was very vague about the last time he had.

'Fin,' I said, feeling increasingly useless, 'would you like the people here to maybe pass a message to your mum? Maybe I could call her, if you want, and say you're fine . . . Well, say you're alive.'

I'd be lying to Fin's mum if I said he was fine. He was the opposite of fine. The the most positive thing I could tell her about Fin was that he was breathing in and out in a regular pattern.

'Dunno where they are now,' Fin said. 'They moved. Lost the address. Stevie knows the address. Keeps forgetting. I'll ask him.'

Well I didn't get much further with this because a man who everyone seemed to know called Elvis, dragging a one-hundred-and-twenty-pound bull mastiff dog on what looked like a school tie, wandered in. Fin stood up, looking very happy to see Elvis, and then Fin, Elvis, the dog (and Stevie) wandered off into the night searching for someone they'd heard had something that they urgently needed. Fin didn't say goodbye. I realized then it was four a.m., I was tired, sad and sat by myself, as the broken-armed woman had fallen asleep. I felt very peculiar.

Frankie, who was playing chess with an ancient man called Major who only had one eye, noticed me sitting there and he shouted, 'You OK, Poppet?'

'Mmm, sort of,' I said.

'What is it?'

I stared at him and scrunched my brow. It was the sort of scrunch that my mother tells me off for as she says it will cost me a fortune in Botox injections when I'm older. Mummy often leans in on me when I'm frowning, points at the wrinkle between her eyes, which between Botox treatments looks like a deep trench a cow could fall into, and says, 'It costs me four hundred and fifty pounds every ten weeks to fill this one in! And you know why? Because when I was your age I used to worry about things that didn't matter. Smile, sweetie. SMILE.'

But sitting here in the homeless shelter, I didn't want

to smile. I wanted to cry. And I knew that the last thing anyone here needed was a snivelling little rich girl sobbing pathetic tears down the front of her Marc Jacobs tipped silk blend cardigan.

'Let's get some fresh air for ten minutes,' Frankie said. 'Excuse me, Major.'

We waited till Clarion was distracted and nipped through the kitchen, snuck out of the back door, shut it behind us, and perched together on the filthy back step in a dirty alleyway, side by side, our knees and thighs touching. It didn't feel awkward, it felt nice.

'What's up? What are you thinking?' he said.

'Aaggagahhah, lots of things,' I said. 'All things. All at once.'

'Like what?' he said.

'I can't say,' I said, 'I'm just thinking about life. But I've not got any of it in any particular coherent structure. It's not like a DNA structure where everything has some sort of meaning. It's more jumbled, like a spaghetti Bolognaise of thoughts. Not that I know how to make spaghetti Bolognaise. I can't cook anything. I can't even ruddy make a cup of coffee. I've had such a silly spoiled life I can't do that. I'm ridiculous.'

'Hmmm,' he said.

'OK,' I began. 'If I had to pick out one thought, I'd say I'm thinking that Fresh Start makes my head feel very full up. Do you know what I mean?'

'Yes.' He nodded.

'It makes me think that there's lots of bits of the world that are quite serious, and my life is destined to be silly and idiotic, and that makes me anxious. And that I don't want to be another Montague-Jones who spends her whole life buying installation art she doesn't understand and putting it in a vault so no one can see it and drinking pink champagne out of thin flute glasses and sponsoring polo events and appearing with a lot of diplomats' daughters in the party section of *Vogue* grinning like I've got a coathanger in my mouth. I want to do something helpful. Like, something really actually helpful? And not just for one night. Do you know what I mean?'

'Yes.' He smiled.

'But I mean it, Frankie! Really, properly helpful. Not like Knute, who keeps handcuffing himself to Virgin Airways planes at Heathrow and messing up thousands of people's holidays and weddings and funerals, then telling the papers he's saving the planet, and the papers saying, "No, Knute, you're actually a ginormous bumhead and we all hope you get run over by a jet." Helpfulness gets kind of diluted if thousands of people think you're a tedious pain in the neck. And everyone thinks that about me now. I read something horrid about myself today in fact in *the Guardian*.'

'Well I don't think that,' Frankie said. 'That stuff in the *Evening Standard* last month was awful. The photos were a complete joke. You were in a stationery shop buying art supplies, weren't you, and the caption said you were a "notorious party animal".'

My mouth dropped open.

'Oh my God, you saw that!?' I said. 'It was an attrocious photo. I looked brain-dead.'

'It wasn't so bad. You looked very pretty. But I had to laugh when I saw you. I said to my sister, 'That's the girl who used to laugh at my naval blazer and ask me where my ship was.'

That alleyway was dark, so I don't know if he saw my face flush red.

'Mmm, you remember that?' I mumbled.

'I do,' he said, 'and Margot remembers Kitten tying her hair plaits to a door.'

'Crikey,' I said, cringing, 'that's unfortunate. Soz.'

'It's fine,' he said, 'we've all had enough therapy now to move on.'

'Stop it!' I squealed as Frankie started laughing. 'Anyway, listen to me,' I said. 'I've not finished. I was telling you about Poppet Montague-Jones making the world better. I want to be in the history books with something awesome under my name! I don't want my Wikipedia entry to be a laughable catalogue of idiotic endeavours ending with a long spell in a foreign prison, or being chased to the country borders by a pack of irate Africans wanting their emeralds back, or dying a lingering death from a disease that makes my ladygarden sprout feathers or fungus then drop off! Do you understand?'

'Ouch!' he said.

'I don't want to meet people like Fin and say, "Mmm, yes, it's sad you've not seen your mother since the 80s and you've clearly got that schizophrenia thing that means there's another man living in your head. Hmm, boo hoo, sad face, whatever, have some lovely soup!" I want to be someone who knows what to do and makes things better.'

'No, I get that totally,' said Frankie, 'I feel the same.'

'Do you? Wow! That's amazing,' I said. 'Hey and do you ever think, Why don't I use the thirty gazillion squillion pounds I'm worth to make things better for everyone? Y'know, spread the happiness? Do you understand what I mean, or do I sound crazy? I should just shut up. I'll shut up.'

Frankie looked me in the eye me with the most peculiar expression, then he began to laugh. 'No don't shut up, carry on, it's wonderful,' he said.

'Oh you're laughing at me!' I said, slapping his knee, 'I'm not being funny. I'm serious. I mean what I say!'

'I know,' he said.

'But do you get what I'm saying?' I said.

'Yes,' he said, 'I feel exactly the same.'

And then Frankie reached out, took hold of my hand and put it to his mouth and kissed it. I looked at him curiously, as if to say, *Did you know you just did that? Frankie, that was like a hand kiss you'd give to someone you fancied.* Well he looked back as if to say, *Yes, I know I did that. What do you want to do about it?* Then I winked at him and he winked at me back and then he pulled me sideways and lightly kissed the side of my face and then I rested my head on his shoulder.

We did NOT snog each other. We did not do anything else at all. In fact we went back indoors soon after.

I don't know what the name is for what happened between us. It was totally odd. Like we crossed a line while both staying on the right side of not crossing any lines. I didn't know how I'd explain it to Striker and Vixen, and was considering keeping the whole thing a secret, at least, until I'd had some head-space to think. But *the News of the World* solved all of that. Because, unbeknownst to us, all the time Frankie and I were talking, a paparazzi phtographer was hiding behind a wheeliebin about fifteen metres away. There was an enormous photo on the front page of the newspaper this morning with the spectacular headline: *ROYALTY IN THE GUTTER: PRINCE AND WILD CHILD'S NIGHT OUT ENDS IN DRUNKEN KERB ROMP.* The photo shows me and Prince Francis looking quite merry, sat on a smelly step, holding hands, with my head on his shoulder. The story says that I'm a notorious party animal and come from a family the Royal Family distance themselves from for their debauched ways. I'm not sure what Mummy makes of all this, but I assume she is very cross. But since her assistant, Matthew, informed her of the news this morning she's not said anything to me. She's been struck mute. Not a single word.

7 P.M. UPDATE

I've been dumped by Kwame Kobina. DUMPED. Well I assume I have. An hour ago my mother pushed a piece of paper under my bedroom door, then clomped off. It was a printout of the email Kwame sent her this afternoon resigning from his job as my tutor and asking for the one hundred and fifty pounds that he's owed. Kwame says he cannot carry on working with me 'due to recent events publicised in today's tabloids that have made his position untenable'. I broke down in tears when I read that and I've been hiding under the duvet with my arms wrapped round my knees, but I've gathered myself together now. I've ripped his stupid, pompous email up into a million pieces and I'm thinking: GOOD RUDDY RIDDANCE, YOU BORING NORK. There was also a note from Clarion expelling me from Fresh Start for bringing the good name of the company into disrepute. Stage Two was putting on a musical at an old folks' home and now I'll miss it. WHAT A SHAME.

MIDNIGHT

Oh God. Oh NO NO NO. OH THINGS JUST GOT REAL. VERY REAL. I just made a 'recovery raid' to the kitchen to fetch my iPhone for the first time today. I've been too scared to leave my room. I've just discovered a terrible, horrific voicemail from a woman called Camilla

Worksop-Smythe at Buckingham Palace. She has summoned me to see her at nine a.m. tomorrow morning 'in order to discuss some urgent matters'.

Oh my God, I've broken the Montague-Jones family. AFTER FOUR HUNDRED YEARS OF BAD BEHAVIOUR THE ROYAL FAMILY HAVE FINALLY DECIDED TO OFFICIALLY THROW US OUT OF THE ROYAL LINE UP. This is the only explanation I can think of. THIS IS ALL MY FAULT. No one will forgive me for this ever. Granny Montague will probably hire a hitman to whack me like in *The Sopranos.* Granny ruddy ADORES being royal.

OMG OMG OMG, I need to pack a bag and get to Heathrow, going via the Montague-Jones vault and getting a few million pounds, then taking the first flight Knute hasn't got cancelled to somewhere like the Congo to live in a forest with a rare indigenous tribe who don't know me, then hopefully get eaten headfirst by an enormous crocodile. It's what I deserve.

MARCH

MONDAY 1ST MARCH

I sat upright in bed sweating at two a.m., three a.m., five a.m. and seven a.m. this morning, hoping this was a nightmare. It wasn't. It was real. Then at eight-thirty-five a.m. a dark-blue Jaguar appeared on the kerb outside 1 Octavia Square, accompanied by a curt-sounding text from Camilla Worksop-Smythe instructing me to get inside as 'punctuality was paramount'.

I panicked as I was still in my Sith Lord dressing-gown, ran to the pile of clothes on my chaise-longue, pulled on black leggings, a long black jumper and some leopard-skin pumps then threw my hair into a bun and ran for the door, only to bump into Mother on the third-floor landing, who glared at me with her five-hundred-metre-death-stare-of-Satan expression and snarled, 'Where do you think you're going exactly? You're grounded until . . . until, well I don't know when. You're definitely grounded NOW I've worked that out. Get back inside your room!'

'I'm going to Buckingham Palace!' I said.

'Oh really, GET BACK INSIDE . . .' she stared, then she saw I was being serious. Her face froze in horror and she said in a low growl, 'Why are you going there?' And then she said, 'Oh God. Oh no. You've not had a call, have you?'

'Yes,' I said, 'I've had a call. From Camilla Worksop-Smythe.'

My mother swayed unsteadily on her feet and her voice seemed to go silent and whiny, 'Camilla Worksop-Smythe? But . . . no . . . oh my Lord. Well this is just ruddy marvellous, isn't it? We're doomed. Not even Kitten . . . not even your ruddy big sister . . .'

'What *about* me?' said Kitten, appearing in the hallway in tiny gold shorts, a pink sports bra and lemon knee socks. 'What have I not done or done that's scandalous.'

'Not YOU,' I said. 'Me. I've been called into Buckingham Palace.'

'Oh GOD,' Kitten said. 'Oh that's big. That is HUGE.'

'I haven't got time for this,' I said, 'I need to go.'

'Right, Mummy,' Kitten said. 'Call Mr Chenowitz now. We might need to start moving money around in case it all gets nasty and there're any legal arguments over what is ours.'

But my mother was stood there mumbling and ashen-faced, holding onto the bannister.

'Mother, dammit, listen to me,' said Kitten. 'Now, have you got any business projects pending that you need the "By Royal Appointment" stamp on? I'm in the middle of selling my "Sports Socks Fit For a Queen" brand to Nepal, I need to rush that through ASAP.'

'We need to check the lease on the house,' my mother mumbled. 'We own it outright, but I think Princess Jocelyn owns the actual freehold tenure.'

'Call the legal team. Call Daddy,' said Kitten. 'Get Granny in a car round here *now*.'

I didn't have time for their howlings, I ran down the stairs and slammed the door behind me. I wanted, no, *needed* to speak to Frankie, but we'd never swapped numbers. I needed to speak to one person who actually knew the truth about what had happened and could help me.

Instead, out of desperation, I called Striker, who was still fast asleep, but woke up very quickly when I told her the gossip and said, 'Well, Popz, I'm not going to lie to you. This is the most trouble you could possibly be in, without actually getting publicly beheaded.'

'Yeah cheers, Strike,' I said, as the car drove down the Mall, which was packed with tourists. Buckingham Palace loomed ahead and I could tell by the hordes of people staring through the huge wrought-iron gates that the Changing of the Guard must be in progress.

'I mean obviously,' Striker said. 'Now I've been on Fresh Start, officially I think that you've been a very bad girl snogging Prince Frankie and you deserve some punishment.'

'I wasn't snogging him!' I said.

'But unofficially,' Striker went on, ignoring me, 'this is the coolest thing EVER.' She was still laughing as I put the phone down.

The chauffeur and I sat outside the gates for ten minutes, waiting for security clearance to go inside. I was starting to feel highly vile now, I wanted to press the electric window and vomit down the side of the Jaguar, but there were already about thirty tourists with their face against the blackened windows trying to see inside, plus three or four men who looked like paparazzi who'd no doubt had a tip-off there was trouble brewing.

Eventually, the car rolled inside the gates and pulled over to a side entrance. A large white-haired man in a pinstriped suit was waiting for me, wearing a disapproving expression. He allowed the chauffeur to open the car door and then he stepped forward and put out his enormous veiny hand. 'Poppet Montague-Jones,' he said.

'Hello,' I said, in what voice my dry throat had left.

'Falstaff Bingley,' he said. 'I'm deputy-head of palace media communications. Thanks for coming in.'

'No, the pleasure's all mine, really,' I said, in tones of heavy irony, 'I'm in really bad trouble aren't I?'

He narrowed his lips at me and said, 'Well that's your choice essentially, Poppet. You can talk about your options when you meet Mrs Worksop-Smythe. Walk this way.'

Falstaff set off, with me behind, through Buckingham Palace. I'd not been there for over a decade. I'd forgotten how enormous and grand the rooms are and how every wall is filled with portraits of the ancestors and gifts from foreign dignitaries, how every corridor has glass cabinets carrying rare *objet d'art* and every lobby has at least one silly-looking Corgi dog wandering about confused, looking for a way out, or one rather ancient-looking Queen's lady-in-waiting walking along waving a check-list, mumbling about packing something into a suitcase to go on some Royal Excursion. I'd forgotten how some parts of the palace smell quite dusty and a little rotten.

With every corner we turned, I dreaded bumping into the Queen or Prince Phillip. I was terrified. Every time a door opened I expected to see Her Majesty standing there with her Mr Whippy white hairstyle ready to thwack me with the royal handbag for making her family the laughing stock of Britain again.

By the time I reached Camilla's office I was tearful and shaking. Falstaff gave two loud knocks on the door.

'ENTER,' shouted a voice.

'May I introduce Poppet Zanzibar Montague-Jones,' said Falstaff Bingley, theatrically, before placing one hand on my shoulder and almost pushing me through the door to meet my nemisis. The door slammed shut and I heard him march briskly away down the corridor.

Suddenly I felt very, very alone.

Camilla was about seventy-years-old, with skin like a walnut, a pea-green two-piece suit, pearls and horn-rimmed spectacles. She was sitting at an antique oak desk in a bay window with large, draped, deep-purple velvet curtains behind her. All of this colluded to make her look a lot like Satan's messenger. Camilla was leafing through a pile of paperwork, marking things with a fountain pen. I could see no laptop or desk computer. It was like an office from the olden days.

'Miss Montague-Jones,' she said, peering at me. 'I should recognize you from the front of the newspaper. Although it was difficult to see your face. If only Prince Francis had been so lucky.'

'I can explain about that,' I said.

'Explanations are not my department,' she said. 'My job is damage limitation.'

'What does that mean?' I said.

'Well,' she said, 'my job spec isn't to nurture or guide the important young royals, y'know, the A list, the ones people care about, no, my job is to swoop in when things have become a mess and clean the mess up.'

I stared at her. I didn't like this stupid old bat already.

'Are you saying,' I said, 'and maybe I'm reading this all wrong here, that I'm a mess that needs clearing up.'

Camilla just stared. That answered the question.

'I think we can both agree that this has been an unfortunate situation,' she said. 'His Royal Highness Prince Francis has had some difficult times recently. This has led him to associate with some unconventional people whom the Palace would rather were confined to history.'

She left another long silence. I stared back at her.

'So my aim,' she said, 'is to eradicate these negative influences in such a manner that will promote and enhance the strong reputation of the Royal Family.'

I was getting slightly riled by her business jargon, when I knew she was simply meaning, *We hate you.*

'Camilla,' I said, 'let's just cut to the chase, shall we? Am I expecting a trapdoor to plummet me into a pit of killer pigs any second? What have you got in mind for me?'

'I'm not threatening you,' she said. 'My aim is to come to an arrangement so the Prince's opportunities to interact with negative influences are diminished.'

'Aaaaaagh! Why don't you just say what you mean?' I said. 'My head hurts. What do you want me to do?'

Camilla gave a small snort of annoyance, then pushed two pieces of paper across the desk at me. The first one I picked up appeared to be a press statement, except the name at the bottom claimed it was written by me.

'I took the liberty of scripting a few words you might want to say to the press,' she said.

My statement, which was a highly wordy and maudlin affair, basically said that I was incredibly sorry for the bad light I'd portrayed His Royal Highness Prince Francis in, what with me being a substance-abuser, a petty criminal, a truant and having severe educational problems. However I could assure them that our friendship was now over, leaving Francis to carry on being the perfect model of modern monarchy, who, if needs be, could lead Britain. My statement finished by asking the people of Britain that if they needed to hate anyone, they should hate me as I took the blame.

'Pah!' I said, throwing the paper down on the desk. 'I'm not signing that. You're insane.'

'Read the second one,' she said.

Well this one was short but exceptionally to the point. It was a form where I agreed to not cross a two-mile seclusion zone around Prince Francis until 2050.

'Is this an ASBO?' I said. 'A royal ASBO? Are you for real?'

'Will you be OK to use a fountain pen, or shall I grab you a felt-tip?' said Camilla. 'I know you have had problems at school. I can sign your name for you if you want.'

'Don't you dare,' I said. 'I'm not signing anything, you insane old goat.'

'Oh, I think you will,' she said. 'By the way, how is your grandmother? Has she still got Westminster Abbey earmarked for her funeral. It would be a pity if it was double-booked that day and she ended up being cremated at Tottenham Crematorium.'

'You complete witch,' I snarled.

'Sign the papers,' she said, pushing them across the desk to me again.

'No,' I said. But I knew I had no choice.

'And what about that adopted brother of yours, Dragon?' she said. 'How did your mother actually bring him into the country from Liberia? I'm amazed the newspapers have calmed down about that. What if a question was asked in parliament? That could be tricky.'

My lip was wobbling now. I was imagining my poor little brother being sent back to the bedbug mattress in the orphanage full of three hundred kids that nobody wanted. I picked up the papers and looked at them again.

Camilla passed me the pen. I let out a little snivel and tears began to fall down my cheek. I took the pen in one hand and leaned forward to take ink from the pot, but I was interrupted by a massive, unignorable THUD. And then some shouting, and then another big THUD and then, 'GET OFF ME, you ruddy old duffers! Don't make me have to take you down! You're all about ninety years old!'

It was Frankie! I leaped from my seat and ran towards the door. Well the vision I witnessed will stay for me for ever. On the corridor floor, being sat upon by three old men in suits, was Prince Frankie.

'Frankie!' I shouted.

'Poppetmpghghgh!' he shouted. 'I heard you were here. Hang on, get off me!'

By this point two yappy Corgi dogs had entered the fray and were trying to rip Frankie's trouser legs. Frankie wrestled himself free of the pile of old men and small dogs and stood up.

'Are you OK?' he shouted at me.

'No!' I said. 'This woman is trying to make me sign this horrid thing that says I'm a maniac. She's giving me an ASBO!'

Frankie eyes narrowed and shouted one furious word, 'CAMILLA!' Then he strode past me into the office and said firmly, 'Right, Camilla. That's the last trick you play like this. You can't run my life any more. I'm eighteen in five weeks' time. I'm an adult. I want you to have nothing to do with me. I'm getting the lawyers to draw up an ASBO keeping you away from my life first thing in the morning. I want you out of my life for ever.'

'Oh don't be so hysterical, Prince Francis,' she said, witheringly. 'The palace does its very best for you.'

'Don't make me laugh,' shouted Frankie. 'This is doing the best for me? You're giving one of the smartest, kindest, funniest people I know in the Royal Family an anti-social behaviour warrant, on the strength of something you read in a tabloid newspaper? And you're doing it without my consent? This is for the best?'

'This girl has past form,' snapped Camilla. 'If I'd had my way I'd have had the Montague-Jones clan wiped from the record books decades ago. They're an embarrassment.'

'Well, you don't have your way. Not any more Camilla,' he said. 'Your time is over. I'm the new generation of Royals and I'm cutting your power supply off. Happy retirement.'

Frankie looked incredibly hot when he was angry, even if I was in the midst of a massive Poppet crisis and really shouldn't have been noticing it. Frankie marched up to Camilla's desk, took the two pieces of paper, brought a Zippo lighter out of his pocket and set fire to them both, then he threw them in the metal wastepaper basket by Camilla's foot. It began to smoke furiously.

'Camilla, I never want to speak, see or hear from you ever again,' he said. Then he span round and said, 'Come on, Poppet, we're leaving.' And he took my hand and we strode towards the door, which would have looked a lot cooler if we'd not collided with a royal Corgi dog and tripped over, and the fire alarm hadn't started sounding, and an old man hadn't ran through with a hand held fire-hydrant and began spraying everywhere with foam.

'Thank you,' I said as we ran down the corridor.

'No problem,' he said, 'I am absolutely livid. I need fresh air. Come with me, I know where we can get some.'

With my arm linked in his, we ran through the palace up a set of stairs to the top floor and into the Royal Ballroom, where the floor was freshly waxed.

'Let's get on the balcony,' Frankie said, opening the large glass doors.

'No, Frankie, the Queen will go mad!' I said.

'The Queen is in Balmoral,' he said. 'Quick, before my security guards catch up with me.'

'I'm shy,' I said. The balcony overlooked the fountains and Hyde Park, where hundreds of tourists always wait for a possible glimpse of the Queen.

'No one will see us,' he said. 'And so what if they do? The papers will be saying tomorrow that you and I are never seeing each other again. Let's prove them wrong.'

'So we're seeing each other again?' I said.

'I hope so after all this,' he said. 'Come on!'

Frankie dragged me by the arm onto Buckingham

Palace balcony, which only ever gets used for Royal Weddings and times when the Red Arrows fly by in formation on anniversaries. We stood there for a while, dangling our arms over the edge, giggling at some of the madder-looking tourists in foot-high Union Jack felt hats, until we heard someone down below shout, 'Prince Frankie!' We'd been caught. We stared down at a small Italian-looking girl in the crowd who was waving and screaming, 'Prince Frankie! Prince Frankie! Prince Frankie!' And then more people joined in and some people were screaming and then someone shouted, 'And it's Poppet . . . um thingy!' and then some Japanese tourists got the wrong end of the stick completely and started shouting, 'Princess Poppet! Princess Poppet!' and then this led to 'Royal wedding! Royal wedddddddddding!'

'No, not Princess!' I shouted. 'Not wedding.'

But Frankie was howling with laughter then and he grabbed me by the waist and pulled me into him and kissed me fully on the mouth, and then we stood there and snogged, totally ignoring that hundreds of people were really screaming – and we looked down and tons of people were filming.

'We are in so much trouble,' I said.

'I don't care,' he said.

'I don't care either,' I agreed. And I meant it. I absolutely don't care about what the newspapers or anyone who doesn't know me thinks about me. I don't care if Poppet Zanzibar Montague-Jones is at the epicentre of a small media scandal, which is updating every ten minutes on *Sky News* as I write this. I think that sometimes you have to forget who everyone else thinks you are and concentrate on who you know you are instead. And for the first time in my whole life I know who I am and I think I'm rather ruddy OK.

TUESDAY 2ND MARCH

Despite my ex-boyfriend, Kwame Kobina, turning out to be a big dull dud who made my life rather intolerable for four weeks with fold-out charts, Venn diagrams, chew-your-fist with boredom lectures and his constant kissing of Boudecia Prendergast's flabby behind on regular basis, it turns out he was an excellent tutor. Today was my first day back at Hampstead Lycée after weeks away and I returned today to find the teachers in a far more jocund mood and my grades in a much sunnier position. I am being entered for all of the GCSE exams – 'Bo' says my progress has left her 'spirited'. Having read *Wuthering Heights* and accepted none of the main characters are called Garfield, Homer or indeed Scrappy-Do, my essays are a lot more coherent. And in Physics today, I actually knew what the teacher was talking about and could concentrate.

Not that I had much to be distracted by. I have been blanked by Blitzen Trapper. She will not say a word to me.

It's BLISSFUL. I can't imagine what she must be mad about? And the funny thing is, her friends Amelia and Bella are all over me like poison ivy rash saying, 'So Popz, when Prince Frankie takes you to Farenheit, do you get a guest list? And if you got married do you think it would be a traditional affair with lots of bridesmaids? You'd probably be looking for girls the same height as you with good bone structure, wouldn't you?' Meanwhile Blitzen sits there with a face like she's been eating lemon rind with Marmite sandwiches for lunch. I almost feel sorry for her. About five per cent sorry.

So, yes, Striker's and my resurgence upon Lycée was joyous. And Vixy was in a good form as the *Evening Standard* is running a large double-page spread feature tonight on Vixen's Sugarspun Visions cupcakes and now Harvey Nichols' foodhall are talking to her about it. She brought me a box to school today with the words *TEEN ROYAL RUMPUS* iced onto them, which was the headline in the *The Mail* today.

When Voychek drove me home from Lycée tonight, we were both laughing at Talk London radio as there was a phone-in about the state of the monarchy and people were talking about the whole balcony snog like they knew me, but half the time they were mixed up with Kitten or Knute or some other aristocrat that was nothing to do with our family at all.

Voychek turned down the radio and said to me, 'It make me mad, Poppet, they don't know your family at all.'

'Oh don't worry, Voychek,' I said, 'I don't care. It's just noise. People talking and talking. None of it's important.'

We sat at the traffic lights for a while in silence and then he suddenly said out of the blue, 'I'm sorry we have arguments, Poppet. Back when I first get job of driving you. I was trying to look after you.'

Well I felt bad when he said that as I could tell he felt guilty and I knew I hadn't been the easiest person to be around either, so I said, 'I know you were, Voychek. I'm sorry for being a pain. And the time I called you Potato Head. And the time I threatened to kick your window. I know I'm not perfect.'

Well Voychek chuckled a bit then and he said, 'I have daughter like you in Poland. Katarzyna.'

'Have you?' I said.

'Yes,' he said. 'She twenty-two now. Live with boyfriend.'

'I didn't know that,' I said. I don't know anything about Voychek. He never tells and I never ask.

'Hmm,' he said, as if to say, *Well, there you go.*

'Do you have a wife in Poland?' I said.

'Hmmm, did, but we split up,' Voychek said. 'So I miss lots of Kat growing up because wife not want me to speak to her. But we good friends now. Speak on phone.'

'Good,' I said.

We drove along in silence for a while. I was thinking about all the times I've shouted, 'Voychek! You're not my ruddy father, Voychek, leave me alone!' And I wanted to say, *Oh my God, Voychek, I've been an absolute dimwit,* but then I thought: No, he is a ruddy annoying Potato Head at times so surely this makes us as bad as each other. So instead I said, 'Would you like a cupcake, Voychek?'

And he said, 'Yes, I like cupcake thank you.'

So then I took some tissues out of my schoolbag and carefully wrapped him the nicest pink cupcake, and he put it in his glove compartment to take home and have with a cup of coffee.

In other news, Kitten and Mummy are in a far more jovial mood with me now that I'm dating HRH Prince Frankie and the paparazzi outside our house constantly ringing the doorbell are there for a cheery reason rather than something horrid. Camilla has sent no more messages and I'm hoping she'll leave me alone now and not invoice Mummy for a new set of purple velour curtains, which apparently took two buckets of water to put out and left her office with quite severe soak damage. Flash thought this was hilarious when I told him about it this evening. Flash says I am in the running to be the best Montague-Jones member ever and he's putting a big gold star beside me on the family tree project.

I've let Flash into a secret that I've not told anyone else yet. I told Flash about the Poppet Zanzibar Montague-Jones Make the World More Ruddy Jolly Foundation, which I'm setting up. Frankie and I made a pact last night over a pizza that, from this summer onwards, we're going to start giving away five million pounds a year each to charity causes. We've decided to make a wholehearted effort to be on the side of good not evil. We also spent a lot of time with breadsticks up our noses laughing like loons, but that's not the important part. I spoke to Mr Chenowitz at lunchtime today and the first thing I want to do is completely renovate the asylum-seeker shelter and build a playpark beside the contaminated land in East London. He said I was insane and he would give me time to come to my senses. I said I would never come to my senses, I planned to live my life being a mixture of wise, helpful, stubborn, and incredibly silly. He groaned when I said that and said, 'I know.'

'Flash,' I said to my little brother as I helped him with his homework in his bedroom, 'how many Kinder eggs do I need to buy your silence?'

'Three a week,' he said, without thinking.

'Done deal,' I said, and we shook on it.

Just then my phone bleeped with a text: U GOING OUT WITH FRANKIE 2NIGHT? IF SO, HOW LATE U STOPPING OUT? STRIKER XXX

So I texted back: GOING 2 FILM PREMIER, LEICESTER SQUARE, BUT HOME BY TEN-THIRTY. WHY?

The reply came: I AM WITH U. OK? I WON'T BE. BUT IT'LL BE LESS TROUBLE.

WHO ARE YOU WITH?

There was an eight-minute pause before the next text. BIZZLE, it said. DON'T FLIP. HE'S CHANGED. HAD HIS TAG TAKEN

OFF! HE SAYS HE LOVES ME! HE'S RECORDING SOME TRACKS. SAID I WUD GO 2 STUDIO AND LISTEN TO THEM.

Well I'd have argued with Striker, but my mother was making a terrific noise downstairs in the hallway, shouting, 'Poppet! Poppet, we need to work out a strategy of how to deal with all this new press attention. There are thirty people and a *Sky News* van camped out on my doorstep and the neighbours are going to lose patience! We need to draft some type of statement!'

'Hmmmm,' I said.

'Look, I've told them you and Frankie are just teenagers and you're only dating,' said Mummy, 'but they keep asking me if I can see you being, somewhere in the future, Princess Poppet. What do you want me to say?'

'OK, I'll come now,' I said.

I'm going to go down now and work on a statement strenuously downplaying any affairs of the heart I have with HRH Prince Francis. We're only ruddy young. I don't want to marry anyone, especially not a proper prince. I mean how hilarious is that? What is this, a ruddy fairy-story? I don't want a gingerbread house or a gang of dwarves following me around either. And I certainly don't want to live in that big draughty house full of Corgi dogs and cobwebs. But I can't help feeling, despite all that, and forgive me for being all girly for a moment, that Princess Poppet Zanzibar Walcott has a rather lovely ring to it. In fact, it sounds rather ruddy lovely. Doesn't it?